Watching

Watching

a novel by
John Fergus Ryan

For Irvin –
with fond memories of
many years of friendship!
John –

John Fergus Ryan
Sept 26, (1997)

Rosset-Morgan Books
A Division of United Publishers Group

Rosset/Morgan Books
A Division of United Publishers Group Inc.
50 Washington Street
Norwalk, CT 06854

Library of Congress Catalog Card Number 97-066299

ISBN: 0-8038-9398-1 (Hardcover)
ISBN: 0-8038-9403-1 (Trade Paper)
Cover Design by Steven Brower
Distributed by Publishers Group West
Emeryville, California

Printed in the United Satates of America.

10 9 8 7 6 5 4 3 2 1

"The darkness is my parish."
Thomas Merton

1.

I am a voyeur and a bi-sexual foot fetishist. I am also a member of the American Association of Retired Persons.

2.

I live in the bourough of Manhattan, in New York City, New York, in the United States of America.

At any given moment there are at least two thousand people here who are bound or otherwise immobilized and strangers are putting alligator clamps on their bare nipples. At any given moment, there are twenty thousand men walking the street dressed as women. At any given moment, there are five thousand men with the sex organ of another man in their anal cavity. At any given moment, there are one hundred thousand women walking the streets, offering their bodies for sale. At any given moment, there are four thousand men bound with ropes and having their ass holes sealed with dripping hot candle wax. At any given moment, there are fifteen men lying in urinal troughs in the mens' room of gay bars, begging for golden showers. At any given moment, there are about one hundred naked men and women being whipped in basement dungeons. At any given moment, there are hundreds of people with the bare feet of others in their mouths.

All of these people are celebrating life.

3.

George Gershwin played the piano at my grandparents' wedding. He was not famous then, he was just a boy who lived in the neighborhood, 14th Street at Seventh Avenue, and played the piano at weddings.

My mother kept the program with a list of the songs he played and she used to show it to me, every now and again, when I was growing up. He performed at the reception for two hours and favored the crowd with NIFTY-NIFTY, MEET ME IN THE BAMBOO GROVE, AT THE SEASIDE WITH YOU, I'LL BE TRUE TO TESSIE, and I WISH I HAD A SISTER LIKE YOU.

I was puzzled by that last title. What kind of a song would that be? I WISH I HAD A SISTER LIKE YOU? Who would be singing such a song? I once tried to look it up in the library but it was not listed there. I wrote some of the major music publishers who had been in business in those days and long after I had forgotten about writing them, I got a letter from Harms Publishing Co, stating they had published a song titled I WISH I HAD A MISTER LIKE YOU, by C. Claude Caldwell, Ben Angel, and T.W.

Ralston Jr., in 1903 and wondered if that was the song I was referring to.

Of course! I WISH I HAD A *MISTER* LIKE YOU! It now made sense. The program was wrong.

4.

I worked for Glinzretti Brothers in the Bronx thirty-two years, making pickle jar lids. I have been retired four months and so far everything is going well. I have a good pension, almost what I made when working, and I have life insurance, health and accident insurance, even dental insurance.

So far, the pension check arrives when it is supposed to but I am holding my breath. The pension fund is administered by the union which is run by the Mob.

It is no secret.

5.

I have a few friends and there are no more than twenty people in all Manhattan who even know my name. Most of these live in my apartment building, in that part of Manhattan called Hell's Kitchen, near West 48th Street and 9th Avenue.

One is Katherine Hoffman, who has no visible income yet does not want. She is too old to be a prostitute, so I have concluded she has investments, since there is never any man in her apartment.

She is given to stating things in the extreme. Yesterday she told me that eighty per cent of the people in Manhattan have AIDS and that it is just a matter of time before it is a ghost town. When that happens, she says, there will be no one around to provide essential goods and services.

There is an actor named Larry who lives on the ground floor. The front door of his apartment is painted red and there is a white star painted on it at about eye level. He is gone much of the time, appearing here and there in doomed theatricals and when he is to be gone for long periods he subleases his apartment. Once he let it to a member of a rock band who conducted sacrifices of live chickens in the bedroom. He left several days before Larry returned from appearing in a dinner theatre production in Nutley, New Jersey, and when Larry entered his apartment, he was met with the stench of rotted chickens and there was dried blood on the counterpane and white feathers all over the floor.

M'Liss Cameron-Pease also lives on the ground floor. She moved to Manhattan from Montgomery, Alabama, ten years ago, to write a novel. At first, she worked on it every day, but then she met and came under the influence of some people who convinced her it was possible to enter a trance and escape from her body and actually hover over it. She spent much time with them and even tried to interest me in their theories and gradually quit trying to write. It was then she discovered cats and took in several of the disgusting creatures and cared for them and then devoted her energy to preventing the use of animals in laboratories and the wearing of coats made of animal fur.

She is, shall we say, a bit over-dedicated. She writes letters to the newspapers, pickets fur salons and even goes out and throws white paint on the fur coats of socialites, most recently on a fur coat being worn by Mrs. Winston Monaghan as she was entering Carnegie Hall. I do not know where she gets the money to live. We who live in the building with her assume she must have wealthy parents in Alabama who support her.

M'Liss is about fifty-five now and wears a dead white cosmetic, something like grease paint, on her face.

Two lovers, Herman and Bernie, live in an apartment at the back of the second floor. Both are in their late fifties, maybe older, and they have been together many years, perhaps as many as twenty-five or thirty. Herman grew up in Albany and Bernie in Manhattan. Bernie works at a gay movie arcade on Eighth Avenue and he makes twice his salary each week from hustlers who pay him off before he allows them to go into the back room of the arcade where there are always lots of men waiting to engage them. Herman does not work and is supported entirely by Bernie.

There is a young man named Bud who lives in the attic, another young man whose first name is Grey, who lives in an efficiency apartment on the second floor and a middle-aged disbarred lawyer named Alvin who also lives on the second floor. He is from Virginia and is very courtly. He lost his license to practice law because he was inept. He never filed pleas in time, indeed never did anything in a timely manner and was never in the courtroom when he was supposed to be. I got this information from M'Liss, in whom he often confides. Alvin is some sort of administrator at an old folks home in Brooklyn. He has a lot of word processing equipment in his apartment and is writing a novel about the aging process or about old people in nursing homes.

There is a young man named Jack who lives in a basement apartment with a young actress. Jack manages a video rental store in Queens, and often quarrels with his girlfriend, whose stage name is Stormy Heather. I once witnessed an argument between Jack and Stormy on the street in front of the apartment building and saw her take off a shoe and try to brain Jack with the spike heel.

So there you have some of the people in Manhattan who know my name. I will introduce others along the way.

I have never married. I have almost no family, only

my cousin Vinnie Blucker and I have never had any of the
family gatherings at holidays that are said to be enjoyable
and necessary for happiness.

This does not bother me for I have learned that unhap-
piness is not so bad.

6.

It is winter, late January. Outside, the wind off the Hudson River is cutting like a knife, but I am toasty warm in my apartment.

The building itself was constructed in the 1880's, one of many like it put up in this part of Manhattan to house the Irish and German immigrants. It is well made, with thick stone and brick and mortar walls. The windows still fit tight, the rooms are big and the floors are made of oak, still smooth and firm.

There is a boiler in the basement which keeps hot water in the radiators and as long as it works the apartment is warm enough to sit around in my pajamas, even when it is below zero outside.

I have several fears, dreads which actually paralyze me if I think about them. One of them is of being without heat in the winter and since heating systems break down all the time it is a certainty that one day, maybe soon, I will have no heat in my apartment.

In the past, I have had the heat turned off because I could not pay the bill and I would slowly get cold then start to freeze in my own rooms. It is terrifying. When I was a boy and the heat was turned off I would get in bed between layers of newspaper and stay warm, sometimes for two or three days or as long as it took for my father to get the heat back on. Newspaper is a great insulator. I used to wear a sort of vest made of newspaper when walking to work as a young man. I wore it under my coat and I stayed warm.

These days, I have a down sleeping bag with a hood that can be zipped up all the way to my nose. That should keep me warm enough to survive if the heat ever goes out. I also have four blankets which I have picked up over the years at the Salvation Army Thrift Store on West 44th at 10th Avenue. Two are thick army blankets and the other two are high quality, made of Merino wool, expensive if you buy them new but I got them, over the years, for three or four dollars each. I kept them in a cedar chest. I grew up feeling secure from the smell of cedar. The chest I have is old and the cedar smell was not too much when I bought it, also at the Salvation Army, but I took it home and sandpapered the inside down to clean wood and brought out the clean cedar aroma, a scent, as I have said, that I associate with safety.

My apartment consists of two rooms and a small kitchen and a bath. My bed is in one room, the smaller of the two, and that is where I keep the cedar chest and the sleeping bag. The other room is a combination living and dining room. I have a television set and a record player and a book case and a small dining table with two chairs. I have some paintings on the wall, all of which I bought at the Salvation Army and one of them is in the style of Edward Hopper and is a depiction of a bleak sidewalk in front of a row of tentaments and it has an EH signature at the bottom. The liklihood that it is, in fact, the work of Edward Hopper is so remote that I have never even thought of having it appraised.

The other thing I fear is illness. I am particularly susceptible to influenza and about eighteen years ago I had pneumonia. I was living on 46th Street then and I had been in my room by myself for a few days with what I thought was a bad cold. I can remember being delerious and I remember my mind racing, tumbling thoughts over and over. A lady in the next apartment heard me coughing and knocked on my door and asked if I was all right. If it had not been for her, I would have died. I let her in and while she was there I coughed up bloody sputum, which she recognized as symptomatic of pneumonia and she got me to the Emergency Room at St. Claire's on West 50th.

After three weeks, the Sister said I was well enough to leave and I was discharged one afternoon in February. It was cold outside but the sun was bright. If you had looked out your window and did not know it was February you would have thought it was a summer day, so bright was the sun.

I should not have tried it, but I started to walk home which was about four blocks away. After two blocks, I was crushed by fears of death, of being alone, and by memories of the pain, the headaches I had suffered. I sat down on a bench. I had on a hat and a brown overcoat and I probably looked like a secure and prosperous citizen taking the sun.

When I got to my apartment, I was almost lifeless and was sweating profusely. I went right to bed and stayed there two days without getting up. The lady next door, whose name I learned was Rose Malone, cared for me until I was able to go back to work.

That was the only time I have had pneumonia. I have had influenza many times, most recently, last winter. It was unlike any flu I have ever had. There was no fever, just coughing and delerium.

Who would care for me now, if I got seriously ill?

7.

I was born with one leg shorter than the other. To be specific, my left leg is one inch shorter than my right leg.

When I was growing up, the other kids teased me, of course, and did not invite me to their parties or to join their games. I tired to overcome the limp by exercise and muscle building and when I was about sixteen, I got into boxing. I used to hang around Stillman's Gym, watching the boxers train and running errands for Mike Jacobs, the fight promoter. Jacobs managed a few fighters and at one time also booked the fights at the old Armory, which is now gone. He encouraged me to train and I did so eagerly, now, I realize, to compensate for my short leg, but then, because I saw myself as a boxer, making lots of money, and maybe, winning a title.

I was big for my age and from using all the weights and the pulleys I developed a big chest and heavy muscular arms. I was good, even with my short leg. I had a few bouts at the gym, nothing special, just pick up fights and I usually won, three times by knockouts.

When I was twenty, Mike Jacobs booked me in a three round preliminary at the St. Nicholas Arena, against Nate

Blenden, a kid from the neighborhood. I now realize I got the fight because Jacobs saw an "angle", a fighter with a gimpy leg. I thought I was getting the fight because I had talent. That was not it. When the card was announced, I saw my name at the bottom "Nate Blenden vs Billy 'The Gimp' O'Leary"

Blenden won by unanimous decision and I boxed in public no more, but that night was the most exciting in my life. The St. Nicholas Arena, it was, and the great Beau Jack at the top of the card.

Although I no longer did any professional boxing, I stayed around the gym. I kept up training and kept myself in shape even after I left school and worked as a messenger for Wolfe and Nagle, the Wall Street brokers. After I started working for Glinzretti Brothers, I used to drop by the gym, put on the gloves, box a little and work out on the bag. I grew older but I kept in shape. I got heavy and slow but even today, I can still throw a punch.

I had just one fight where I got my name on the card but that nickname they gave me stuck. Ever since that fight, I have been known as Billy the Gimp. A man cannot get into any classy circles or meet any high class people if he is introduced as "Billy the Gimp".

My bad leg and my nickname have held me back. I think both are responsible for the life I have led, always by myself, sometimes lonely, sometimes wishing I knew somebody to have over for supper.

8.

Before I retired, I left my apartment in the daytime only because I had to be at the factory at seven-thirty in the morning to begin an eight hour shift stamping pickle jar lids out of sheet metal.

Now that I do not have to be anywhere during the day, I stay inside most of the time, never going outside until it is dark. I do not even go out to shop for groceries. Bernie gets what I need when he goes to the store, once a week, and he picks up small odds and ends for me at the Korean deli on the corner of 48th Street and 9th Avenue.

I am especially fond of those tiny Cuban bananas they sell along 9th Avenue, tiny little things, they are, and much sweeter than the usual size banana.

During the day, I stay inside, dozing and listening to phonograph records which I have bought at the Salvation Army. I have about two hundred albums, all in excellent condition.

I read about three books a week. I like biographies, especially those of entertainment personalities, and I read some poetry. But not just any poet. My favorites are Thomas Hardy and William Butler Yeats. I also read the

TIMES every day and sometimes try to work the cross-word puzzle.

Afternoons arrive and slowly pass.

I eagerly await sundown and the fall of darkness.

Every night, I go to one of the adult movie arcades on 42nd Street. I miss a night only if I am sick with a fever or if it is too cold to walk through the snow.

I leave my apartment building about nine p m, turn left to 9th Avenue, then south to 42nd Street, where I turn left at the Empire Coffee and Tea company, and head in the direction of Broadway.

Eighth Avenue in that part of town is mostly titty bars and hookers. Broadway is mostly dingy souvenir shops. Forty-second Street is porno movie houses and Africans selling charms.

It is supposed to be dangerous but I have never felt it to be.

There are two arcades I patronize most of the time. One is on 42nd Street and is called the Bon Joy. It has nine booths with coin operated movie projectors and only shows hard core bondage movies made in Germany. The quality of projection is excellent and the place is always spotlessly clean. It is a small scale operation, with bondage video tapes for sale displayed on one wall and bondage magazines on the other. There is a shelf just inside the front door where copies of bondage newspapers, containing advertisements from people who want to meet others who are into bondage, are stacked for sale.

To the right, just inside the door is a counter where sits an impressive looking gentleman, whom I have decided is from India. He is so large and so dignified and looks so

high born that I have named him The Maharajah. He has
been making change for me, changing ten dollar bills into
tokens, most nights for the last seven or eight years, yet
he has never spoken a word to me, nor I to him, beyond
the first few visits when I handed him the ten dollar bill
and said "tokens".

Everything about the Bon Joy is clean and new looking. It is the only one of the arcades in this area of which
that could be said. Wait! I must take that back. There is
another arcade, the palace of all arcades, across the street.
It is called the Crystal Video Theatre and it has four floors
and a two hundred seat movie theatre and sixty coin operated video machines and a live stage show featuring naked
women. It, too, is very well kept, but I do not go there,
for reasons of which I am not sure, but which are probably
connected with my being happier in smaller and quieter
places.

The movies at the Bon Joy are truly hard core bondage, showing behavior between people that is sometimes
too grim to watch. They run the same movies for months
and months at a time and I have watched all nine so many
times I have come to think of those who appear in them
as friends and I have made up biographies for each one,
and I know their faces well enough to recognize them in
the street, if we were to meet.

Here is a brief description of each of the nine movies
now showing at the Bon Joy:

One: a woman wearing a cat costume, black vinyl with
a long black tail and a cowl with ears that stick up, whips
a naked woman tied to a wall with her hands over her
head. The movie starts with the naked woman already tied

to the wall and her back already red with welts. It is never clear why the woman is wearing the cat costume or why the naked woman is being whipped. The whipping is unmerciful and absolutely real. The movie runs twelve minutes and I do not see how the woman being whipped can survive, so intense is the punishment.

Two: A man knocks at the door of an apartment and is admitted by a young maid servant, who shows him into the room where the "mistress" is waiting. The mistress is furious because the man is ten minutes late and she orders him to strip and lie down on his back on the floor. He does. She pulls her chair close to him and digs the spike heel of her shoes into his breasts, almost standing on them. Then she beats his flaccid penis with a short leather whip.

Three: The movie opens with a fat young man, naked, tied facing the wall with his hands over his head and his legs pulled apart and tied. From a distance of ten feet away, a woman wearing a black leather vest and black leather boots is shooting darts into his hips with a blowgun. She laughs, inserts the darts in the blow gun, then PFFFFT! and another one is hanging in his buttocks. The places on the man's hip where the darts have entered begin to bleed. Soon, his hips are covered with blood. The woman wearies of the game with the blow pipe and sets it aside, picks up a ping pong paddle and starts swatting the man's hips with it, driving the darts in deeper.

Four: A man, dressed in black dancing slippers, tight, black pants, a white silk shirt and full cut, leg-o-mutton sleeves with ruffles, is whipping a naked woman, who is on her knees, facing away from him. He orders her to pull her legs in so her buttocks will be higher. She complies. He whips her methodically, appearing bored with the work. After a while, he stops and she is taken into the arms of another naked woman who has been off camera. The two women kiss and make love for a few minutes, the second woman remarking to the first, "Heinz has torn you to pieces." This is spoken in German with an English subtitle. The first woman returns to the position on her knees and the man resumes whipping her.

Five: This one is allegedly filmed live in a famous Sado/Masochistic bar in Hamburg. A man selects two women who are sitting at a table and they are taken to a back room where they are stripped and tied together. The whole movie is devoted to the mechanics, as it were, of tying two women together. There is no action beyond this.

Six: A man is in a room with a naked woman who is standing on her tip toes with her hands tied over her head and attached to a ring in the ceiling. Beneath her feet is a stack of popular magazines, among them *Der Sturm.* He lashes her hips with a cat-o-nine tails, stopping now and again to slip one of the magazines out from under her toes. After he removes three or four magazines, she is off her toes and swinging from the hook in the ceiling. He picks up a thin cane and lashes her in a frenzy. Then he lowers her to the floor, unties her, drops his pants and she gives him a blow job.

Seven: This one shows a man in a green suit entering the room in a brisk, military fashion with a whip in his hand. Two naked women are bent over a railing. He gives each a few swats on the ass with the whip then attaches ropes on pulleys to them and pulls them up off the floor. He pulls more ropes and their legs are spread apart. He lowers the women, attaches other ropes to them, pushes a throttle and the women are bent into arcs.

Eight: A naked woman is tied to a wheel, her legs spread apart. The wheel is turned until her head is at the bottom of it. A man in a white coat pierces her vaginal folds with a surgical instrument and inserts a metal ring in her flesh then he repeats the proceedure until there are three rings there. The wheel is turned again until the woman's head is at the top and it is noted that she has a ring in each nipple. The man hangs weights on the rings and pulls her nipples down.

Nine: A naked young man is tied to the wall with his hands over his head. A naked young woman sits on the floor in front of him and is masturbating him with her bare feet. Another woman dressed in black leather is overseeing the activity and warns the girl on the floor, in German, not to permit the man to have an orgasm. He does, which infuriates the woman in black leather and she lashes both the man and the other woman with her whip.

The other arcade I often visit is called the Sultan Adult Book Store and it is at the other end of the spectrum from the Bon Joy.

You enter it off 8th Avenue and the first thing you see is a display case containing a meager assortment of sexual appliances. A woman, maybe thirty, perhaps some sort of Gypsy, sits behind the display and will sell you the tokens you need to use the video machines in the back. This place is shabby, it smells of urine and the disinfectants they use to clean the primate cages in small town zoos. There are a few video tapes for rent, a few adult magazines, their pages stapled together.

If the Sultan had to depend on the merchandise on its shelves for profits, it would have gone under long ago. The merchandise is just window dressing. The real purpose of the Sultan is to provide a place for people to have "quickie" sex relations. Behind the display case and the Gypsy woman is a long hall with private video viewing booths on each side. Each booth has a chair in it and a door that can be locked from the inside. This is more window dressing. The partitions between the booths have holes in them, some big enough to walk through, some big enough to stick an arm through and some just big enough to peek through.

The Sultan is a voyeur's paradise. One can watch others having sexual relations, either by looking through the peepholes or by actually entering the booth with them.

I will go into detail later about what goes on in the Sultan, that urinous smelling, sticky-footed Temple of Enlightenment.

9.

Other than those who live in my apartment building, the only people I know well enough to talk to are the other older men who regularly visit the arcades. I may have given you the impression that I am the only one who goes to the arcades every night but that is not true, for there are many men just like me who stay in the arcades for hours every night, hoping they will be lucky, that they can watch through a small hole in the wall as attractive people on the other side have some sort of sexual union.

There is actually a sort of comraderie, for instance, at the Sultan, among the older regulars. They visit with each other in the darkness when there are lulls in the action and share experiences and I even know the names, the first names, that is, of several of them.

Last night, I was at the Sultan along with four or five older regulars and we were all watching and waiting to see if the young man with the long blonde hair that hung past his shoulders would make a connection with anyone he considered worthy of him, when one of the regulars, a man I know as Jimmy, slipped up beside me in the darkness and said, "Ted's gone!".

I knew Jimmy well enough to know Ted was the fellow he lived with. Ted came in the Sultan once in a while. Everybody liked him, he was a gentleman, polite and courteous.

"Where'd he go?" I asked.

"He's gone! Killed himself!"

I was shocked. Ted was one of the group. Both Ted and Jimmy, roommates, mind you, both old men, would come to the arcade together and share the gropings and the peepholes.

"Killed himself?" I asked.

"Hung himself!" said Jimmy.

He told me the story. He and Ted were in their apartment getting ready to watch one of those old movies on their VCR. Johnny Sheffield in *Son of Tarzan*, it was. Jimmy was popping corn, pouring Cokes when he heard Ted in the next room moving a chair. The telephone rang. Jimmy heard Ted answer it. "No," said Ted. "They don't have this number anymore. They have a new number. If you'll hold on for a few minutes, I'll be happy to look it up for you in the directory." Jimmy said he heard Ted give the party calling the new number, then he heard the chair being moved again, then he heard Ted sigh but he thought nothing about it, then he heard the chair fall over and he went into the next room and there he saw Ted hanging from a steam pipe in the ceiling with his bathrobe tie knotted at his neck.

"I got him down as fast as I could!" Jimmy said, "but it was too late."

10.

Bud, who has the attic apartment, is Clam Manager at an Italian seafood restaurant and makes a lot of money on the side giving whippings to masochistic men.

He is thirty, keeps his weight down and exercises daily, running along the Hudson eight or ten miles a day. He is a big man with blonde hair and a handsome face, who advertises his services in some of the bondage magazines and in the little newspapers they keep under the counter at newsstands.

I have talked to him about his work. He makes two appointments a day and his customers include young men, old men and in between. He services them in his apartment.

Bud thinks of it as just a job. He considers himself some sort of actor, like in a pageant. He tells me he meets the client or customer in black leather pants, black boots, a black leather jacket with no shirt, a black leather motor-cycle cap and dark sunglasses.

A session lasts about an hour and is tailored, so Bud tells me, more or less to the customers' wishes. Usually, it is a whipping, while handcuffed and while wearing tit clamps. Some customers get a golden shower.

An hour with Bud costs a hundred dollars. He has a few women clients but he does not charge them. "I whip them just for the fun of it!" he says.

Bud makes two hundred dollars a day, sometimes more when he is willing to extend himself. Two sessions a day is best, Bud says, because after two, it is impossible to keep a hard on, which is his big selling point, since Bud says he has ten inches, uncut.

Two hundred dollars a day! I get outraged by the amount of money some people make these days. Me, I had to work six weeks at Glinzretti Brothers, back in the fifties, to make two hundred dollars.

11.

Last night, I went to the Bon Joy and lingered in the lobby, looking at some magazines containing photographs taken in a nudist colony. I look at such photographs once in a while but the "goody-goody" atmosphere you find in a true nudist colony becomes boring.

I went back where the booths are, put a few tokens in the machines, saw segments of all nine movies, then I went to the vending machine, bought a Coke and stood in the dark, hoping someone interesting would come in.

As my eyes became accustomed to the darkness, I made out another man standing a few feet away. I could see he had long, stringy blonde hair and wore glasses and a black knit cap. He was wearing jeans and a thin zipper jacket and had a pack on his back, like he might have been a camper. He moved closer to me and I could see his glasses were held together at the nose by adhesive tape. He got even closer and started mumbling something, trying to communicate with me.

I could see his face clearly now, the dirty long hair, the gaps in his teeth, his patched eyeglasses, his dirty clothes.

He had "CRAZY" written all over him.

"Fuck this arcade!" he said. I ignored him and took a sip of my Coke. "They ain't nobody here," he said. "Fuck this arcade!" He swung his bag around from back to front and reached in it and took out a sandwich and started eating it.

"You brought your lunch?" I asked. He patted the pack, now hanging on his chest and said, "Lunch ain't all I brought! You know what else I got in here?" "What else?" I asked. "A quart of gasoline!" he said.

He was crazy, all right. Running into crazies is a risk you run, going regularly to the arcades. Religious crazies mostly, who are opposed to the free-wheeling sex on the screen, and crazies like this man, who brought gasoline with him.

"I'm going to torch this place" he said. "Since I got back from overseas, I can't get my rocks off unless I'm in a burning building."

What should I do? I thought about going out to the lobby and telling the Maharajah there was a dangerous looney inside and then leave it to him to handle.

The man walked away in the darkness and I found myself distracted by a group of college boys who came in and I forgot about him. I went into a booth and spent another dollar in tokens watching my friends on the screen then I left the booth and started walking toward the entrance.

I heard a man inside one of the booths talking out loud. "Take it, Baby!" he was saying. "Oh, Baby! Oh, Baby!" he repeated. I saw that the door of the booth was ajar. "Take it, baby!" he was saying, in a tone of voice that indicated he was really having a good time. I wanted to

34

see what was going on and I pushed the door open slightly. Suddenly, the door was opened from the inside and I was yanked in. It was the crazy, in the booth by himself. He grabbed me by the back of the head and tried to pull my face down into his crotch. I simply cupped both hands and clapped them with all my strength up against his ears. The man collapsed and slumped to the floor.

As I left the Bon Joy, I stopped to tell the Maharajah that some man who had a quart of gasoline in his pack had passed out in one of the booths.

12.

Sometimes I ride the subway just to look at feet.

It was about ten-thirty at night, last Saturday, I think it was, and I was sitting on one side of the subway car, looking at the feet across from me. I became aware of a young woman, in a tight black dress, no hose, and black suede shoes with high heels. She was sitting next to a man about thirty-three who was wearing a pair of crepe soled brown leather shoes that came to his ankle bone. He was wearing a checked flannel shirt, double knit pants in a plaid and a tweed sports jacket and carrying some books and he had a shoulder bag in his lap. I made him out to be a graduate student or maybe a new Ph.D. and as I listened to him and the girl talk, I realized I was right. He was talking to her about some poet he liked. Soon, another young man sitting a little bit away on my side of the car hailed him and they started talking about a mutual friend, Al, who was at Columbia on a tenure track. The second man said he worked in the library at Columbia. Then he told the first man, "I was putting some books on the shelves today and I saw your new one. Congratulations!"

The "new book" turned out to be a collection of po-

etry the first man had written and which had been published, as I made it out, by Columbia, and had been
favorably reviewed by someone at the Columbia
newspaper.

I looked at the "poet", sprawled on the subway seat,
in his mismatched clothing, some of it appropriate for
working as a lumberjack, some for herding sheep in Scot-
land, some for cleaning the attic, his attractive girlfriend,
taken by his stature as a published poet, her leg thrown
across him, and I wondered to myself if this poet had ever
heard of the people I call poets.

13.

Bud, my young neighbor who makes a good side income applying the lash to other men, told me he was expecting a client at two o'clock and asked me to let him in if I heard the bell.

On the off chance, I asked Bud if I could watch. He thought about it a moment then said, "Yes".

The man arrived at the front door on the appointed hour and I let him in and showed him up to the attic apartment, where Bud was waiting in the doorway. He was wearing black boots, black leather pants, a black leather jacket, black sunglasses and a black leather motorcycle cap. He was holding a short black leather whip in his hand and was leaning against the door frame with one of his legs crossed over the other.

The client was about thirty, not very tall and a little overweight. He wore a yellow sweater, khaki pants and a pair of shoes that looked a little like dancing slippers. He saw Bud in the doorway and stared at him, saying nothing. Bud pinned him down with his eyes, like a hawk would eye a mouse helpless before it.

Bud spoke.

"Strip!" he ordered.

The man started to undress in a terrified frenzy. When he was naked, Bud ordered him to crawl into the bedroom on his hands and knees. The man started to comply and Bud walked along beside him, flicking the man's bare ass with the whip.

I followed them into what looked more like a gymnasium than a bedroom. There was a sort of vaulting horse and a large thick mat covered in plastic, inside a sheet metal tray with sides that came up about three inches.

Bud ordered the man to stand and put his hands behind his back. Bud handcuffed him then put tit clamps on his nipples and the man writhed in pain. Bud turned him around, pushed him down across the vaulting horse and started beating his buttocks with the whip. The man seemed to like it and kept calling Bud "Master".

The rest was what must be a standard workout. Bud took off his leather clothes, one piece at a time, with short intervals between each item, and forced the man to perform oral sex on him then give him a rim job and suck his toes.

I noticed the man did not have an erection and Bud commented on it, demanding to know why he was not excited.

"I'm TOO excited, Master!" he said.

Bud spent another thirty minutes with the man, then took off the tit clamps and while the man was sighing with relief, put them back on again.

I noticed that Bud did not have much of an erection either, but I presumed it was the consequence of a busy week at his trade.

Bud took off the tit clamps and the handcuffs and ordered the man to lie down on the plastic covered mat on his back. Bud sat on the man's chest and masturbated, shooting his load in the man's face.

"Open your mouth!" Bud ordered. The man obeyed. Bud stood up and started pissing, aiming for the open mouth and hitting it. The man swallowed the urine and I noticed he started to have an erection. Bud kept on pissing in his mouth and the man's hand became a blur and he reached a climax, gasping and bucking as he continued to swallow Bud's piss stream.

Bud noticed the man's excitement and sneered at him.

"So, you're nothing but a little piss queen!"

"Yes, master!" said the man.

Bud ordered the man to get up. He handed him a towel and ordered him to sop up the urine in the metal tray. He did so.

The man must have been there before for he picked up his pants, pulled a one hundred dollar bill out of a pocket and handed it to Bud.

The man was covered with urine and semen.

"Get dressed and get out!" said Bud.

"Yes, Master!"

He left and Bud turned to me and held up the hundred dollar bill and smiled.

14.

Last night, about 10:30, Bernie knocked on my door and then I opened it, he put his finger across his lips and whispered, "There's a prowler in Alvin's apartment! Herman and I heard him making noise in there!"

"Maybe it's Alvin!" I said.

"He's out of town," said Bernie. "Come upstairs and listen to the noise."

We went upstairs to the back of the hall and stopped in front of the door to Alvin's apartment. Someone was inside, opening the drawers, moving the clothes in the closet, obviously looting the place.

I knocked on the door. "Alvin, is that you?"

There was no answer. I knocked again. "Alvin! What's going on in there? Is that you, Alvin?"

No answer. I asked again, "Alvin, is that you?"

"Si!" came an answer from the apartment.

Bernie ran into his apartment to call the police.

The police never came, or, at least, never let us know they were there. Alvin returned the next afternoon and Bernie and I were there when he unlocked his apartment door. It was just as presumed. The rooms had been looted.

Clothes were thrown all over the floor and the contents of drawers were tossed here and there.

A window in the bedroom was open. It had been forced from the outside by someone standing on the roof, someone who had got there from the roof of the apartment building next door.

After Alvin put things back in order, it appeared that the only thing missing was a pair of running shoes. He repaired the broken window then nailed it shut and put a piece of two by four at the top to keep the window from being raised.

15.

My cousin Minnie Blucker, the only relative I have left on Earth, called to tell me she was retiring and to invite me to her farewell party.

Minnie has worked for Yak Brothers for thirty-three years. She is a remnant folder, her only joy being the discovery of new materials, new patterns and new colors in the big cart of fabric scraps from the cutting room floor.

Yak Brothers makes automobile seat covers and decorator pillows. Now a multi-million dollar business, it was started in 1946 when Axel Yak opened a small automobile trim shop and started making seat covers on a treadle powered sewing machine.

He was an artisan and he prospered from the first and twice moved to bigger buildings before he settled in a factory that covered a city block and where he had over a hundred employees. Even then, he kept the records in a bellows file and figured the profit and loss from notations he kept in a black notebook he carried in his shirt pocket.

My cousin Minne is a good employee. She never asks for anything, is never late and works even when Axel Yak or one of his sons is not watching her.

As they both grew older, Azel Yak came to consider Minnie a good example to the others and pointed her out to the textile salesmen who came around in silk suits. Sometimes he advanced her money to get her husband Harvey out of jail. Harvey refinished hardwood floors for a living but he was an alcoholic and they depended on Minnie's income.

When Axel Yak died three years ago, the trade journals described him as the elder statesman of the automobile seat cover business and recalled that he had cut the first terry cloth throw, had perfected the one size fits all stretch seat cover and had pioneered the use of giberboard quills to anchor the front seat covers in four door automobiles.

Harvey Blucker died about the same time, leaving Minnie at the mercy of Axel's son Irving, who took over the management, hired accountants and started to trim the payroll.

I told Minnie I would be very happy to come to her retirement party and I wrote down the date and then called Jack Sidney, at Yak Brothers.

Jack was Irving Yak's brother in law and had worked at Yak Brothers since he was fifteen. I asked Jack, whom I had known many years, why Minnie was retiring so early and to get some details about her farewell party.

Jack told me that "Mr. Irving", as he called him, had decided Minnie was too old to be productive, she sat down too often and was sometimes too stiff in the joints to reach into the bottom of the remnant cart so he had told her it was time to retire, but because his father had always considered her loyal, he was going to give her a farewell party at the plant.

The party was to be held in the showroom, I learned, a windowless chamber I had visited before, reached by walking past tall stacks of finished seat covers packed in dusty boxes, then through the sewing room, into the pillow room, where the air was filled with floating particles of kapok, and into the dark, hot warehouse where rats played under piles of raw materials, ate the poisons set out for them and then died in inaccessible corners.

One wall of the showroom was hung with cardboard miniatures of automobile seats, displaying samples of the styles and patterns of seat covers the company manufactured, each one ornamented with a glittering silver plastic welt at the seams.

At one end of the show room there is a bar made of quarter inch plywood and stained walnut then varnished. A large hasp, of the sort used on garage doors, had been screwed at a slant across the back of the sliding doors on the cabinet where the liquor was kept, and it was always locked.

Jack Sidney told me "Mr Irving" had agreed to pay for food and drinks for ten people, no more, and he told Minnie to invite five friends at the plant. After two days of trying, she was able to find five people, including me, who said they could come and she gave the names to Jack. At Irving Yak's insistence, one of the names was removed from the list because Irving thought its owner was a Communist.

Someone in the shipping department heard of the party and suggested Jack Sidney start a pot to buy Minnie a going away present. Jack made the first contribution with three dollars out of petty cash. A total of fifty-three dollars was collected and given to Irving Yak's secretary to buy the gift and she chose a set of matching aluminum cookware with anodized blue lids. She kept what was left over and bought herself a good lunch, or so Jack Sidney told me.

Every day, when her shift got off at four-thirty, my cousin Minnie would come into the city sales office and sit in a sagging chair by the door and read THE AMERICAN LEGION magazine, U S NEWS AND WORLD REPORT and FIELD AND STREAM until five minutes until five when she would walk to the corner and get on the bus that took her home.

Once a month, with an authority to do so that seemed to be rooted in the old days of Axel Yak, she would take the magazines home with her.

Jack told me she ignored the magazines during the last week and asked everyone who came near her in the city sales office if they knew Irving Yak was throwing her a party.

On Friday, her last day, she came to work dressed up. She wore a crepe dress that had once been blue or purple, sturdy black shoes open at the toe and a corsage of gardenias given her by the Sisters of Saint Teresa, for whom she did volunteer work.

She had had her hair done.

At five-fifteen, the party assembled in the showroom. Two of the friends Minnie had invited could not be there and Jack Sidney apologized for the absence of "Mr. Irving".

While Manny the Caterer unloaded the dinner from his truck, Jack unlocked the cabinet behind the bar and took out a fifth of bourbon. Minnie who did not drink, said that just this once, she would.

Two folding metal tables had been opened up under Jack Sidney's direction and covered with white paper. Minnie, me, Jack Sidney and Rose Pollitt, Irving Yak's secretary, sat at one table and Minnie's two friends sat at the other.

Manny the caterer provided a salad, choice of dressing, turkey on toast under a cold cheese sauce, frozen green peas, clover leaf rolls and a chocolate pie that tasted like molasses.

After the plates had been cleared away and Minnie had started to drink a second glass of bourbon and Coca Cola, Jack Sidney stood up and said that all of them, especially "Mr. Irving" were sorry Minnie Blucker had decided to retire, they hoped she would visit them often and that this little gift was a token of how much they were going to miss her.

Minnie opened the package and said the pans were nice but she was hoping it would be a window fan and did Jack suppose she could exchange it. Rose Pollitt said she was sure Minnie could exchange it and told her where she had bought the pans.

Minnie said she would miss everyone and that she hoped some of them would come to see her and that she loved them all and that she had asked the Lord to bless them.

She took a sip of her drink and began to cry.

Jack Sidney laughed and asked her what she was going to do with all the spare time.

The party broke up.

I walked to the corner with Minnie and stood there with her, holding the box of pans, while we waited for the bus. It was the old familiar corner but everything looked different to her, she said. She had never been there at night before and the whiskey had made her sleepy and a little dizzy. Automobiles raced by and she looked at them and asked me if I thought there might be Yak Brothers covers on the seats. She gazed dull-eyed at faraway neon signs and looked up at the stars.

After a long time, the bus arrived and we got on it, me still carrying the box of pans. We sat in a seat near the driver and Minnie caught his attention and told him Yak Brothers had thrown her a party. He was from another culture and did not understand.

I saw her into her apartment and set the pans on a table in the kitchen then I hugged her and kissed her cheek and said goodbye.

It began to snow as I walked to the subway. Soon, I was in the Bon Joy and talking to my friends on the screen, telling them that life was sometimes very sad and one of them, a stout young woman wearing only black shoes, turned to me and said in German, "It is so, my friend!"

16.

It is intensely cold as I walk along Ninth Avenue tonight. I would guess the temperature is down to twenty degrees or less, but I am dressed warmly and do not suffer.

I see the street people, sleeping over the grates or in the doorways or lying on the sidewalk with a layer of cardboard under them and coats and blankets over them. Their heads are covered, their feet are covered and they look like enormous cocoons, only, come Spring, they will not burst forth as butterflies.

None of these street sleepers will see Spring. The cold will get them first. When I was a boy, there were always cartoons and jokes about bums sleeping on park benches and the notion was vaguely comical. Now, it is different. Now, there are thousands of people in New York City who live on the streets and who crawl into packing cases or into vacant buildings, like alley cats, to spend the night.

These people are almost all mental cases and I did not see such on the street when I was a boy because, then, they were kept confined in mental hospitals where they were fed, clothed and bathed and kept safe.

Somewhere along the line, in the past twenty years, I

would say, they started turning these people out of the asylums and giving them some pills and instructions for taking them regularly.

This was a social workers' notion. Give them mind altering drugs and they will be all right on the outside. Of course, it was nonsense. They do not take the pills, they just drift into the streets where they do the best they can for themselves, which is usually no better than sleeping in a cardboard box.

I occasionally try to talk to street people. I have never succeeded. They are always too disturbed to participate in a conversation.

Thanks to the social workers, they are condemned to walk the streets, sleeping here and there, eating what they can find in garbage cans, until, in a short time, no longer than the length of the first winter, they freeze to death during the cold nights.

I have seen the city trucks, gathering the frozen dead from the streets on bright winter mornings.

17.

I was coming out of Grand Central Station yesterday when I ran into Carl.

He lived in my apartment building about ten years ago with an advertising copywriter named Brecht, who kept him as a slave. Carl loved it! He used to sleep on the floor beside his master's bed, with no cover, even on the coldest winter nights. Carl did not have any clothes. Brecht would not allow it. Whenever it was necessary to take him out of the apartment building, for instance, to go to the dentist, Brecht would allow Carl to wear some of his clothes, which was all right, since they were both about the same size.

It was awkward, even in a place so filled with exotics as was our apartment building, to go to Brecht's apartment for a little wine and cheese and see Carl, naked, and curled up in a corner, keeping to himself, staying out of the way unless Brecht barked an order at him. One Christmas Eve, several of us were in Brecht's apartment for fruit cake and eggnog, and while we were there, Carl was kept locked in a small cabinet and he made not a sound.

Once, Brecht dressed Carl in some of his old clothes and they took a taxi to the office of some sort of beautician who pierced Carl's nipples and inserted gold rings about the size of a five cent piece in each one. Then he pierced the end of his penis and inserted another gold ring, this one about the size of a twenty-five cent piece. Carl was then made to dress and Brecht took him back to their apartment, where he was again undressed and made to sleep on the floor.

It took weeks for the punctures in his flesh to heal and he had high fever some of the time.

It was rumored that Brecht later took Carl to the same beautician and had him branded on the hip with a red hot iron. We never found out if this was true.

Carl loved his life. He used to bear the lashings with no complaint and Brecht even trained him to wait for permission before having an erection.

Then, one day, Brecht moved out, taking everything except Carl, whom he left curled up on the floor. When we learned Brecht was gone and Carl abandoned, we got together some clothes and a little money and gave them to him and he, too, left.

I had not seen Carl in ten years when I ran into him at Grand Central Station. He had a suitcase in his hand and was wearing clothes that looked like they had been provided by a rescue mission.

Carl said he was moving to Nebraska to be slave to a wheat farmer whom he had contacted through an advertisement in DRUMMER magazine. The farmer had a barn with livestock in it and Carl was to stay in the barn, again with no clothes on, sleeping in a stall with the cattle.

I asked Carl where he had been since I last saw him and he said in New Jersey, kept as a slave by a stockbroker who had a large house with a dark basement. Carl said he had once been tied up in the basement, hanging by his wrists about a foot off the floor for three days, with no food.

"How did you go to the bathroom," I asked. "I just went," he said. The stockbroker came down to the basement at last, with a powerful water hose and washed everything into a drain in the floor.

"Do you still have that ring in your schlong," I asked.

"I now have FOUR!" he said.

18.

I have mentioned the people who live on the street, those who sleep over the grates at night and whom I claim are all mental cases who were let out of the asylums when the social workers discovered mind controlling drugs.

For a time, I thought there might be exceptions.

Last summer, I got up early several mornings and walked from my apartment to Central Park, to Columbus Circle, and sat on one of the benches, taking the early morning air.

Each morning, I went into the Pax Restaurant at Seventh Avenue and Fifty-seventh for breakfast, and the first morning, I saw a young man, maybe even a boy, on the sidewalk. He was thin, dressed in shorts and a short-sleeve pullover shirt and was barefooted. I only saw him from the back, that first morning. He had very long brown hair that stood out all over his head like the fuzz on a dandelion.

A street person, he was, a young man with no fixed address unless it was Central Park, two blocks away. I am sure he slept there, perhaps on the ground during the warm nights. He seemed so friendly, although, mind you, I did not see his face the first few days, or at least, not clearly.

He looked, how shall I put it, desirable. Why was this thin, attractive dark-skinned boy living on the street? Why did not someone take him home, if only for one night, if only to bathe him and perfume him and get him in the sheets, even if for one night?

I saw the boy every morning for five or six mornings, always facing Seventh Avenue, just standing there or sitting on the curb, always barefooted. I noticed the second day that his legs were caked with dirt and he was scratching his head with his fingernails. Still, I could not understand why a young man, so basically attractive, had to live on the streets. I could understand why some of the street people, old, heavy men wearing two or three overcoats and carrying a sack filled with dirty clothing, would be ignored, but I could not understand why this young man, whom I had begun calling Giraud, had to fend for himself. I thought for a moment one morning of asking him to come into the Pax Restaurant and have breakfast as my guest. I did not because I realized the staff at Pax would not like it and because I realized, too, that Giraud must be long unwashed. I continued to watch him from my breakfast table, never seeing anything but his back.

The last morning I was at the Pax Restaurant, I saw him from my table, sitting on the sidewalk, his bare legs even more caked with dirt and scratching his head in a frenzy. I paid my check and stepped outside and looked at him closely. He was now standing up. Never had I seen him begging, he never spoke to any passer-by, but in spite of this, I had in my hand a few dollar bills which I was going to give him if he caught my eye.

I got close to him and he turned and I saw his face.

He was a beardless boy with no teeth in his mouth, his eyes those of a mad man.

There was no hope for him. I knew as I walked away that come the winter, he would die.

19.

I was walking on Christopher Street and passed a man who was offering used bondage equipment for sale. He had put up a little table just off the sidewalk and it was stacked with an assortment of tit clamps, handcuffs, and leather paddles.

He nodded at me as he stamped his feet in the packed snow to keep warm.

"Where could I go to watch this stuff being used?" I asked him.

"Ther're lots of leather clubs," he said. "Try Cell Block Twenty-Two."

I shook my head.

"They won't let a man my age in places like that."

I pulled the collar of my overcoat up around my neck and walked on.

20.

I have been going to the Bon Joy so long I feel I know personally all the actors in the movies. The Bon Joy, you will remember, is where they show nothing but bondage movies made in Germany and they have been showing the same nine, now, over a year.

It is very cold outside, there are a few people on 42nd Street, those few fighting the freezing rain and the slippery streets. Inside the Bon Joy, it is warm and clean and cheerful with the blue skinned man I have named the Maharajah presiding at the counter with massive dignity.

I get five dollars in tokens from him and start back to the row of video machines. On the way, I pass a young boy and a younger girl, high school students, by the looks of them, who are examining the porno magazines in the rack on the wall. I stop and pretend to look at them myself, so I can observe the couple. He takes down a magazine devoted to foot worship, as it is called, color photographs of men and women sniffing and kissing and licking bare feet.

He shows her the magazine and they look at it a moment together, she nods, he smiles and they take it to the

Maharajah to pay for it. I turn to watch them and my heart almost bursts with happiness.

I enter a booth and insert a token. It is movie number one, the woman in the cat costume who is whipping the woman tied to the wall.

I have watched this one so often I have given the characters in it names. The woman in the cat costume is Ilka and her victim chained to the wall is Magda. Why are they doing this? I ask myself. Why the cat costume? Why is Ilka being so unmerciful to Magda? How did Magda get in this dilemma? Why did she allow herself to be tied and whipped? These questions puzzled me until I invented an explanation for the relationship of Ilka to Magda. The cat woman, Ilka, I have decided, is a professional disciplinarian, available for hire. Magda was having an affair with the husband of Hilda, whom we do not see. Hilda has hired Ilka to punish Magda. How she managed to overpower Magda and put her in chains is not clear. Perhaps it involved the assistance of two or three strong men, not seen, but in Ilka's employ. They abducted Magda as she was walking alongside a river, say, in Hamburg, and took her to Ilka's chamber.

That explains it all, even why Ilka wears a cat costume, even a cat face mask with whiskers. What Ilka is doing would be called kidnapping and assault by the authorities so she must disguise herself to avoid problems with them.

So, Ilka is unmercifully flogging Magda simply because it is what she does for a living, simply because she has been hired to do it by a jealous wife. What is Ilka thinking to herself as she lashes Magda? Has not Ilka had affairs with married men, herself? Might she not find herself in the same position Magda is in, one day, when another angry wife hires some other disciplinarian to punish her?

What is happening on the screen? I do not remember seeing this part before! Ilka has stopped flogging Magda, whose back is badly bruised, even bleeding in places. Ilka is putting on a glove, one yellow glove that comes up to her elbow. Now she picks up a yellow hose off the floor, a long yellow hose, and with no preliminary, sticks one end of it up Magda's ass. She is going to give Magda an enema! How is it in over a year I have never seen this segment of the movie? Have I always switched the channel before it came on? It must be.

Ilka steps back and we see the other end of the hose is connected to a faucet in the bath tub. She turns on the tap, full force, and we see Magda, her hands tied over her head, start to react from the pain of the cold water entering her bowel. The water is coming in with great force, straight from the tap. How intense must be Magda's pain!

Magda begs Ilka to stop the enema (in German) and Ilka just lays the lash on Magda's back all the harder. Ilka then removes the hose from Magda and moves a large metal tub over to her. Magda releases the water and it flows into the tub, thin, brown sewage.

Ilka, still wearing the yellow glove, dips her hand into the tub and bathes Magda's bleeding back with the warm liquid.

This is bewildering! Why is Ilka going to these extremes? There is no evidence of sexual excitement on the part of either woman. What about Magda? What is she thinking? Does she realize she is being punished because of her love affair with the married man? Did Ilka, upon

meeting Magda, say to her, "You are going to be punished
for your affair with Herr Schmidt? Is Magda hoping for
some intervention, from the authorities or from her friends,
that will end the torture? Or is Magda—could we even for
a moment consider—enjoying the torture? Could she have
hired the cat woman, Ilka, to perform the sadistic acts
upon her?

After watching the entire film, I stick to my original
thesis, that a jealous wife has hired the cat woman, Ilka,
to punish her husband's lover. It makes sense, even the
enema, which is just more punishment, after all.

I try to imagine how this would end. Will Magda be
released? She is too battered to go home and care for her
wounds. She would have to go to a hospital, she will need
high quality care, just to live, if I am any judge of the
severity of her punishment. How will she feel toward Ilka?
She will want to kill her, I imagine. Will the police ultimately be involved?

I need not concern myself. The film goes on to the
end then starts over again. These two lives have been entwined like this over a year. They will go on. It is a movie,
there is no need to try and predict how it will all end. The
punishment will go on and on and on and in the end, no
one will have to answer for it.

I push the button on the video machine and the film
on the screen changes to the one where the naked fat boy
or man is chained to a wall while a woman shoots darts
into his hips with a blow gun. What an odd sexual activity,
I say to myself. Where, for instance, did the producers of
this film get a real blow gun? Aren't they used only by
African pigmies? Did they get one from them? The blow

gun actually works. You can see the feathered darts coming out of the blow gun and lodging in the man's hips. He flinches each time one hits him but it should be no more painful than the daily injection of insulin diabetics give themselves. I will admit I have not watched the entire movie, even though it has been showing over a year, like the rest. I have decided, however, that the fat young man is named August and he works at a truck factory in Munich. I can understand his willingness to submit to having darts shot into his hips. After working all day at some dull task, perhaps sewing the canvas tops for truck beds, he needs something to release the tension, so he visits Mistress Erma in her studio loft, pays over a few marks and lets himself be stripped and chained to the wall. There is no sexual aspect of the relationship between August and Mistress Erma. August never gets an erection and never has body contact with her. Perhaps he believes he is a base person, somehow unworthy and for that reason he hires a woman to stick darts in his hips. I cannot be sure.

I push the button again and again, passing over some of the other movies, and stop at the one where a naked woman is hanging upside down and a man who looks like a Nazi submarine commander, black turtleneck, black blazer and a black naval officer's cap on his head, is piercing her labial fold with a surgical instrument and inserting a metal ring in it. He has already inserted three. I watch as he forces a sharp pointed tool against the underside and pushes it through.

The woman, whom I have named Irmagard, is surely drugged. It is a medical proceedure, not a sexual experience, no evidence of thrill, everything is all business. I have said that Irmagard is surely drugged and I say so because she does not wince when the sharp instrument is pushed through her flesh.

Irmagard is a waitress or perhaps a hairdresser in what used to be East Berlin, where life is incredibly pallid, dull and conventional. She crossed into West Berlin and was abducted by agents of Heinz, a businessman, a degenerate, who gives sex parties in his apartment. He has naked women, pierced such as Irmagard, shackled to the walls for his guests' enjoyment.

The whole concept of piercing is unfathomable to me. It is commonplace among males who are into bondage and discipline. It is always the slaves who are pierced, so I gather, usually rings through the nipples and a ring through the head of the penis. Women are pierced, as was Irmagard, through the nipples and through the vaginal folds. I assume the rings are made of some precious metal, maybe even gold, else how would they not cause irritation and infection? I am puzzled by the actual insertion of the ring. How are the ends of it joined? Are they just pulled close together, as close as possible, or are they actually joined by some heat process? I have never looked at a ring in a nipple close enough to see how it is done. If it is to be done for a lifetime, surely a goldsmith must be on the scene of the piercing to weld the ends.

How does one with a metal ring through his breast nipple explain it to his doctor, or to friends at the beach, or to his draft board? I can see how it would be very beneficial to report to the draft board with a ring in your penis. I should think one so ornamented would be declared unfit for service within a few minutes.

Are not ringed people often seriously injured trying to have sexual intercourse? Does not the ring create pressure on a penis when an attempt is made to force it into a tight opening?

I have heard that Prince Albert, husband of Queen Victoria, had a ring through his penis.

I press the button and move on. Here is Dr. Hoyt! That is the name I have given to the man in the green suit, whom I see every time I come to the Bon Joy. He is a German, of course, like everyone else in the nine movies they show. He is about fifty, a stocky man with glasses and reddish hair combed back from his face. He has on a green suit, green as in the color of corn shucks, light green, it is, and from the cut I am sure it is one hundred percent polyester.

Dr. Hoyt is the name I have given him because it sounds German and sinister. I have watched his movie many, many times and tonight, I have punched the change button and it appears on the screen as it is just beginning.

I put two dollars in tokens in the slot to insure I will see the entire movie, uninterrupted. It begins with a shot of two bare behinds, two attractive women, naked, bent over some sort of bar. Dr. Hoyt enters. He walks briskly, all business, as he comes into the room. An attendant, a man in a white turtleneck and black pants, hands Dr. Hoyt a cat-o-nine tails, and the doctor gives each bare behind two efficient cuts with it, two each, one on each hip. Dr. Hoyt sits down at a desk, and starts studying figures on a piece of paper. He studies them carefully then rises and beckons to the attendant. Dr. Hoyt gives him some instructions and the attendant brings one of the women to him.

It is Betty, an English girl living in Berlin because there, she can sell her body in exchange for drugs, or so I have imagined. She is buxom but not unattractive. The attendant ties her hands to a rope hanging from the ceiling then he brings over the other woman and ties her hands to the same rope. Dr. Hoyt is sitting at the desk, studying the papers in front of him. The attendant announces to Dr. Hoyt that the women are ready. For the next few minutes, the attendant, under Dr. Hoyt's direction, fastens chains to the feet and waists of the women. Then Dr. Hoyt starts wrapping each woman in heavy rope, circling every bare spot with what looks like ship's hawser. Finally, he is finished and he orders the attendant to hand him a length of thin cane. He draws it back, intending to cut Betty across the breasts with it. He pauses, realizing she is covered head to toe with heavy rope and would feel nothing. He sets aside the cane and goes back to his desk and starts slowly making calculations with a compass and a slide rule. He scribbles notes on a paper, smiles to himself, then orders the attendant to remove the ropes, all of which takes time. Dr. Hoyt takes an electronic calculator from his pocket and continues his computations.

I have seen all this before. I push the button and watch the movie where a man who is dressed like a Cuban adagio dancer is whipping a woman on the floor. He whips her a few minutes then allows her to have sex with another naked woman who has been lounging on a divan in the same room.

21.

Times Square, the area around Forty-second Street at Broadway, is crowded with people even on winter nights. The grand old movie theatres on Forty-second, the Empire with its high arched facade, the Amsterdam, the Times Square Theatre with columns across the front, the Lyric and the Victory, where I used to go as a boy to see actors like Jon Hall and Leo Gorcey and the Bowery Boys and William Boyd as Hopalong Cassidy, are all closed now, the entrances boarded over and African vendors are squatting on the sidewalks, selling charms and potions.

There are musicians on the street, people who entertain by playing songs on oil drums and tap dancers and three card monte games going on along the sidewalks in front of the adult arcades. The only stores open sell shoes or electronic gadgets imported from Hong Kong.

There is a Bible act everywhere you turn. One man who preaches in the area should have his sermons silenced by the authorities on the grounds they are obscene. His big pitch is that homosexual behavior is against God's will and he is always shouting something like, "Man was not intended to take into his mouth the penis of another!". There is a Muslim in flowing robes who yells "Kill Faggots!" through a bull horn.

Sometimes I see another preacher, an earnest young man in a suit and tie, who sets up a flannel board on an easel to help him in his campaign against sin. He looks intelligent and speaks well. I cannot imagine anyone in this area buying the nonsense he preaches.

22.

There is a poster on the wall of the Sultan Arcade advertising a coming attraction titled OLGA, QUEEN OF THE ESKIMOS, which it says is about a beautiful young Eskimo princess who gets lost in the trackless snow and gets raped by her own sled dogs.

The poster has been up two years that I know of. Once, I asked the Gypsy woman at the counter when it was going to be shown and all she said was "Coming soon!" and took a long drag on her cigarette.

One man who hangs around the Sultan told me once it was actually booked but got cancelled when the Society for the Prevention of Cruelty to Animals threatened to protest.

23.

I once saw Rodgers and Hammerstein standing in front of a theatre on Broadway. About 1947, it was. Both men were wearing bow ties and double breasted suits. I think they were wearing hats, or maybe, holding hats in their hands.

Living in Manhattan, you see famous people every day, every time you go out on the street. I have seen famous people from President Truman to Frank Buck, the man who brought back the wild animals. I have seen hundreds of famous people but my greatest thrill was the day I saw Rodgers and Hammerstein.

Whenever I hear the waltz from CAROUSEL it makes me feel like I am soaring through the sky.

Bow ties and double breasted suits! I used to dress like that, back then. I wish you could have seen Times Square in 1948, for instance. Everybody was dressed up! Everybody wearing a suit and tie!

And everyone, man or woman, wore a hat!

24.

They began showing eight new movies at the Sultan last night and I dropped by to see them.

The first is set in a hospital room. A man is in bed, a nurse enters and tells him she must take his temperature, per annum. The nurse turns out to be a man dressed as a woman, who inserts his engorged penis in the patient's ass. The patient objects, the nurse becomes aggressive and the patient gives in. Later, the patient fucks the nurse in the ass.

Number two: It opens in a coal mine, six or eight miners stripped to the waist, are mining coal. There is a cave-in. They are trapped without food. Time passes. One miner, a burly Negro, has a lunch pail filled with sandwiches. The others beg him for part of a sandwich. He agrees to share his sandwiches with the men in exchange for sexual favors. The Negro starts to fuck one of the miners, the others get in the spirit, and start fucking each other. Eventually, they are rescued, with the sandwiches uneaten.

Number three is set in a luxurious apartment. Two women are sitting on a sofa. They talk. One strokes the other's breast. In the next scene, they are naked and in bed together. One takes a battery-powered dildo from a drawer and inserts it in the other.

Number Four: A young man about eighteen is reading a specialized newspaper and sees an ad from a man who wants to meet a boy looking for a father figure. The next scene shows him at the door of an apartment. The door opens and an older man is seen. He tells the boy to come in. Cut to a scene on a sofa. The boy is saying, "I have this problem." "What is it, my son?" asks the older man. "It's my penis," says the boy. "During the night, it gets hard and I fondle it and I shoot off on the sheet!" The older man is shocked. "You mean you shoot off all over your clean bedding?" "Yes, sir!". "That's disgusting!" says the older man. "You're going to have to be punished for that! You're going to have to suck my dick!" The young man does as he is ordered. From there, they go into mutual activity.

Number Five: A man is planning a birthday party for his room mate. He wants to give him a gift, an evening's sexual encounter with a new, fresh young man. He calls up an agency specializing in providing such, and asks them to send over a few boys for him to interview. They start arriving. He "interviews" them by having sex with them. He interviews four, makes his selection, and the scene cuts to the birthday party at a grand hotel. The gift is presented.

Number Six: A man and a woman on a sofa. He is wearing a U S Navy uniform, she is dressed in a plaid kilt and a matching plaid tam-o-shanter. She wants to go down on him. He lets her.

Number Seven: A gang bang. Four men and four women. They change partners until each has been serviced by all the others. The movie ends with the women voiding on the men, who are lying on the floor.

Number Eight: A four hundred pound woman is seen tending a baby in a crib. Close up: It is not a baby. It is a grown man wearing a diaper. She changes his diaper, powders him and then nurses him on one of her enormous breasts. She then gives him a blow job.

Another typical bill at the Sultan. The movies change about every ten days. Each one lasts about twelve minutes. For one twenty-five cent token in the slot you get ninety seconds of viewing.

Men watching the movies in a booth usually masturbate and shoot their load onto the floor. After a while, the floor becomes sticky. This gives rise to the name "Sticky Foot" for the less well run arcades, those where the floor is mopped once every three or four days.

At a well run arcade like the Bon Joy, they have a man who mops the floors all the time.

25.

This morning, I went out on Ninth Avenue and bought a copy of *The New York Times*. A headline on the bottom of the front page caught my eye. UNION LEADER IN-DICTED IN THEFT OF PENSION FUNDS. I scanned the article. "Glinzretti Brothers. . . . manufacturers of pickle jar lids. . . . business agent of the local. . . . embezzled pension funds. . . . District Attorney estimates twenty million lost on mob controlled resorts. . . . retirees loose all pension benefits. . . ."

It was what I had been afraid would happen. I was even expecting it. I was done for. My pension gone, too old to find another job.

As I stood at the newsstand, stricken by what I had learned, a young man who lives in the neighborhood, a person in the arts or the ad game, came up to buy a paper. He must have noticed how I looked. He asked if I was OK. I mumbled something about having to look for a job.

"You need a job?" he asked. "Go up to the Metropolitan Opera House! They're looking for a Russian diction coach!"

He left, running for a bus, his shoulder bag slapping against his hip.

26.

My pension is gone. All I have coming in is around five hundred dollars a month from Social Security. I went to the District Attorney's office and talked to the prosecutor handling the case against the business agent who stole the money. He said I could sue him to get what I had coming from the pension, make him pay it back to me out of his own pocket.

Absurd! Did he really mean what he said? The business agent has no money. Besides, he will be in jail for a few years and will not be able to earn any.

I have six thousand dollars in the bank. It was four thousand when I started. That was ten years ago, when my aunt died and left me what she had in Postal Savings Certificates. She must of had them fifty years. I did not even know there were any Postal Savings Certificates in existence by now. I invested the money. I put it in the bank and have been letting it grown there for ten years.

That is how I happened to have six thousand dollars.

It should last me a year, assuming I take out five hundred dollars a month. I went to the Welfare office to find out if I was eligible for anything from them. I asked about food stamps. The answer was 'No', I had too much money in the bank. The woman at the Welfare office used some term, something called 'spend down', meaning, once I had spent all my money in the bank, I could reapply for Food Stamps.

I have enough money to live on a year, if I have no emergencies, such as getting sick or having to move to another apartment. I can make it a year. Maybe I will not live that long. After all, I am what they call a Senior Citizen, a term I despise.

Enough of that! I am on my way to the arcade! I think I will stop at the Sultan, just to see if there is anything going on there. I think the filth might cheer me up!

Snow falling, very cold, night time but bright as day from the lights, the neon, the open shops. I feel pretty good about things, right now, something will work out. I have always really believed that, as far as my life is concerned, things work out for the best.

I actually feel cheerful at this moment. I think I will stop at Lindy's and get some potato salad, maybe a piece of cheesecake.

I walk along, the snow is not a problem. I have on rubber overshoes, I do not worry about slipping. I am feeling good, then—then—I see a person. I cannot tell if it is a man or a woman, but I recognize it as a human form, sleeping, or unconscious, or maybe dead, in the doorway of a shop. It is stretched out, covered all over with a blanket and some coats and I see a layer of newspaper under the blanket.

A movement on the sidewalk catches my eye. I see, in the neon light, a young Black man, crawling into a cardboard packing case. I watch as he tries to seal up the open end with newspaper and masking tape.

I look around and see others, some men, mostly men, but what appear to be two women, old, haggard faces, sleeping on the sidewalk, maybe over grates where the heat comes up from a basement, all in deep sleep, their blankets and shawls covered with snow.

A flood of depression washes over me. I suddenly feel too cold to go on. Were these people once like me, employed at a steady job? Did they too once have pensions?

Is this the end that awaits me?

27.

My money is not going to last a year, as I had hoped. I planned to take five hundred dollars a month from my savings and add it to the five hundred plus I get from Social Security. I have been without my pension now for three weeks and I have withdrawn seven hundred dollars, money I had to have to keep my existence up to the level I was used to.

The bad thing about going to the arcades is I spend about fifteen dollars a night in them. Say I go out twenty nights a month and spend fifteen dollars a night on the movies alone, not to mention the sandwich I usually get on the way home, that comes to three hundred dollars a month, money which I no longer have.

Most of the arcades sell tokens to be used in the movie machines. They cost twenty-five cents each, are made of brass, are about the same size as a quarter and have something embossed on them, such as a naked woman or just a bare breast.

Arcade patrons who have families, wives or girlfriends, dare not accidentally get home with some of these tokens in their pockets because of the explanations it would require.

When a patron is ready to leave and still has three or four dollars worth of tokens in his pocket, he has to dispose of them somewhere. Sometimes, he will give them to the man behind the counter as a tip, and he can redeem them for cash out of the till. Giving him a tip will make him well disposed toward you, once he learns to recognize your face, and that can be very helpful in case there is ever any trouble from the vice squad or from crazies. "I've never seen him before," from the man who runs the arcade will often be all that is necessary if there is a problem with minors—who should not be there in the first place—claiming they were molested in the dark.

Another thing a patron can do with his extra tokens is hide them inside the arcade until the next time he is there. This is not as easy as it sounds. Old time arcade loungers such as me know all about hidden tokens. You can tell an experienced habitué of the arcade as soon as he enters. When his eyes have grown accustomed to the darkness, he will start sweeping the tops of the vending machines and the ledges formed by two by fours with his hand, looking for stashed tokens.

It is almost impossible to hide tokens longer than a day, because everyone patronizing the arcade spends their free moments looking for them and because the man who runs the arcade comes in once a day, during the slowest hour, turns up the bright lights and looks everywhere a token could possibly be hidden.

Since I am now reduced, the importance of hidden tokens has grown very large in my life. The first thing I do now is look for them. A pencil flashlight is required and also the willingness to stand on chairs to reach along the edges.

I used to give whatever tokens I had left to one of the loungers with whom I had shared the evening. No more! Now I take them home and put them on top of my bureau for use the next night. I now hunt for hidden tokens with an intensity I do not think is equalled. Last night, I found seven dollars worth, hanging in a cloth bag behind the plywood paneling at the Bon Joy.

28.

Larry, the actor who lives on the ground floor, heard I had lost my pension and came to my apartment to tell me he was sorry and told me to come to him if I needed any help along the way. He said he was doing pretty good these days, money to spare, he said and things would get better in the spring because he had a part in a production of OKLAHOMA to be done in New Jersey. It was going to run two months, he said, and he was going to play Ali Hakim, again.

I thanked him and told him I thought I could make out about a year. He was surprised, he had no idea I had anything put by. We visited awhile, I played some old records, some dance bands from the Forties, Bunny Berrigan, I CAN'T GET STARTED WITH YOU, Hal Kemp, GOT A DATE WITH AN ANGEL, music like that, and he said, let me take you to dinner tomorrow night. Asti Restaurant, he said, off lower Fifth Avenue. Asti, he said, is where all the opera stars go, where the waiters sing opera. I told him I knew all about it, I told him I had been there three or four times, years ago, with Frankie Rosenthal.

He made a reservation and the next night we took the subway down to Washington Square and walked the few blocks to Asti.

It was very crowded, everybody was happy, singing, raising their glasses. The waiters sang opera and even the owner got up and sang something.

I ordered the steak cooked in cognac, something Larry recommended, and it was delicious.

Can you imagine my surprise when I saw Dr. Hoyt sitting two tables away! Dr. Hoyt, you will remember, is the name I have given the man in the green suit who appears in one of the German bondage movies I have watched several nights a week for over a year, the one who was so impersonal, more interested in his slide rule calculations than the naked women he intended to torment.

It was him, I was sure of it! There was no question it was Dr. Hoyt, he was even wearing the same green suit. I was so excited by his being there! I asked Larry to excuse me and I went to his table, interrupting his dinner, and said something about being a great fan of his. I called him Dr. Hoyt. "May I have the pleasure of shaking your hand?" I asked. He was confused and appeared ill at ease, and told me I had made a mistake. He was not Dr. Hoyt. I am afraid I behaved like a fool. I told him it was all right, I was a fan, he could relax with me. I watch your movie three times a week, at least. He became emphatic, he was not Dr. Hoyt. I was mistaken, he said. He asked me to excuse him so he could return to his trout. I apologized and went back to my table.

Larry asked whom it was I had been talking to. I told

him the man was a film star I had seen many times in bondage movies, but he had claimed he was not.

I then realized why he had not admitted to being Dr. Hoyt. The movies he appeared in were not held in high esteem, perhaps, by people like me. Maybe they were even illegal. Maybe he would be subject to arrest if it was discovered he appeared in bondage movies.

Dr. Hoyt finished his trout and left abruptly, colliding with four waiters seated in office chairs with wheels on them, pretending to be men rowing a boat.

Larry and I stayed at Asti awhile longer, listening to the singers and observing the diners. The others, all fans of opera, appeared to be having a good time, but it seemed to me their gusto and their gaiety was artificial.

On the subway back to 52nd Street, it occurred to me why Dr. Hoyt had been so abrasive. The name Dr. Hoyt was one I had given him! Of course, his name was NOT Dr. Hoyt! Dr. Hoyt was just the name I had been calling him in my mind for the past several months, just as I called the women Mitzi and Erica and Magda and Gerta.

I went to sleep that night without visiting Forty-second Street, confident I had met Dr. Hoyt, whatever his name was.

29.

I now realize it was a mistake, a foolish mistake, to accost Dr. Hoyt in the restaurant last night. Of course, it was him, but I should have realized he would not want to admit to being the star of a pornographic movie. He is probably under surveillance by the authorities, anyway, those who selectively prosecute people who make and distribute pornographic movies, especially movies with as much diabolical machinery in them as is in those of Dr. Hoyt.

It was a mistake and I am now paying for it. A man followed me home from the Sultan last night, just one day after I foolishly addressed Dr. Hoyt in the restaurant. I am sure Dr. Hoyt put the man on me, and ordered him to follow me to find out if I am an officer of the vice squad.

An Asian, it was, a tall, thin man from India or Pakistan, with a crazed look in his eyes. He said nothing to me in the Sultan but I saw him watching me. When I left, he followed me home up Ninth Avenue and when I got inside my apartment, I turned out the light and saw him through the window, standing on the sidewalk across the street. He was not dressed in warm clothing and when I looked out the window a few minutes later, he was shivering and blowing on his hands.

An hour later, I looked out and he was not there.

30.

The Pakistani, whom I have named Mr. Khan for easy reference, was outside my door when I started to the Bon Joy tonight. He was dressed for a long, cold night and had a pack on his back and was holding a large thermos bottle in his gloved hand.

When I started down Ninth Avenue he took up following me, ten or so yards behind. Once in awhile, I would look over my shoulder at him and he would catch my eye and turn his head.

He had a contorted face that frightened me and I concluded that Dr. Hoyt had loosed a friend on me, one he kept for the purpose, and that he had ordered him to assassinate me.

I reached the Bon Joy, entered hurriedly, bought tokens and scurried to a booth and locked the door. When I saw Dr. Hoyt on the screen, I told him about the man who was following me. I assured Dr. Hoyt that I represented no threat to him and had greeted him at the restaurant because I was a fan. Of course, nothing I said was heard by those on the movie screen. Talking to my friends on the screen is exactly the same as directing prayers to Heaven.

When I left the booth, I looked for Mr. Khan, but he was not there. When I left the Bon Joy and stepped out onto Forty-second Street there was no sign of him and I relaxed and thought I might be mistaken.

I started up Ninth Avenue and he appeared behind me and followed me all the way home. Once inside my apartment, I again turned off the light and looked out the window and there he was, in a down jacket, gloves and a navy watch cap, ready to pass the night virtually on my door step.

I had noticed the light on in Larry's apartment and I walked across the hall and knocked on his door. He let me in and I told him about Mr. Khan, with his face of a fiend, who was following me. I explained all, I told him I had recognized Dr. Hoyt at the restaurant where he took me to dinner, as he would recall, and that it had been a mistake to let Dr. Hoyt know I had recognized him and Dr. Hoyt had set Mr. Khan on my tail, surely to kill me at the most opportune moment.

Larry looked out the window in his apartment and saw Mr. Khan. He suggested I call the police. I told him that was impossible because I did not want to involve Dr. Hoyt, a man who had given me some exciting moments on the screens at the arcade.

I told Larry this was a problem I would handle myself.

31.

M'Liss Cameron-Pease got out of jail yesterday, after serving ten days for throwing paint on the fur coat of Mrs Winston Monaghan, while Mrs Monaghan was wearing it into Carnegie Hall.

To celebrate, Bernie and Herman had a little party in their apartment.

Katherine Hoffman was there along with me, Larry and Alvin, the disbarred lawyer. The man we know only as Bud, who lives in the attic and who makes good money whipping masochists, was not there. He left, actually fled in the night, three days ago, leaving his rent paid up until the first and all his belongings, including the leg irons, the tit clamps, the handcuffs and the whips. He had been on duty in the kitchen of the clam house where he worked when two men entered the back door, walked through the kitchen to a small private dining room and shot some big shot mobster in the head as he lifted a forkful of spaghetti to his mouth. They left by the back door only this time they saw Bud as he was running down the alley and now they are looking for him to silence him before he identifies them. At least, that is what the police think.

Bernie and Herman had some wine and cheese and some little cakes covered with chocolate icing, some olives, some crackers and a few dips.

M'Liss looked bad and she said it was terrible being in jail, locked up with drug addicts and prostitutes and street crazies and she said it was unjust to do that to her. "I was jailed for my beliefs!" she said.

Katherine Hoffman, who always carries every discussion to an extreme, agreed with her and gave some examples of others jailed for their beliefs, such as her friend Mischa, from Morocco, who was jailed for his belief that the books in the library belonged to him, and who took home around a thousand of them without first notifying the librarian.

Bernie asked M'Liss if she had learned a lesson, being in prison ten days, he asked if she was going to throw paint on another socialite and she said, 'No!'. Prison was too terrible, she said, to risk going back there because of some overt act. She would continue to write to law makers and the newspapers but no more would she throw paint on those wearing furs to dramatize her position that killing animals for their pelts was murder.

"Besides, I have a new interest now," she said. "Something I realize is far more important than animal rights."

"What is it?" we all asked.

"I have become interested in Hunger!" she said.

32.

Three nights ago, the burglar came back, this time to murder. The police are sure it was the same man who had been in Alvin's apartment, the one who answered "Si!" when we called to him, because of his modus operandi. He got in by way of the roof again, this time entering the apartment of Bernie and Herman, both of whom were there, sleeping.

He awakened them, made them stand up then put the muzzle of a gun at the back of Bernie's head and pulled the trigger.

The bullet, a large calibre, according to the police, tore through the back of Bernie's head and came out through his mouth, splitting his teeth into shards with the force of shrapnel, into Herman's eyes, and beyond, some embedding themselves in the woodwork.

They held Bernie's funeral today, while repairmen sent by the landlord dug bits of teeth out of the door frame and repainted it. Herman is in the VA Hospital, blind, and now eligible, they say, for some sort of disability benefits.

33.

Mr. Kahn loitered around my door and then followed me to the arcade every night for the next week. He never said anything to me but when our eyes met, he glared almost pure hatred at me, and sometimes spat contemptuously.

I was beginning to wonder if he was, in fact, an agent of Dr. Hoyt. I also realized I had to stop calling the man on the screen Dr. Hoyt, at least when trying to link him with the insane looking Pakistani on my tail. Hoyt was not his name, of course, and if I ever had to involve the police, I must be careful not to refer to "Dr. Hoyt", or they will think I am insane.

As preposterous as it must sound, I began to grow used to Mr. Khan. In fact, I thought of him as a protector. If Dr. Hoyt had assigned him to follow me and rub me out when the time was ripe, surely Mr. Khan would intervene if I was jumped by muggers or one of the out and out crazies who walk the streets among us.

Then, I came back to reality and told myself something had to be done about Mr. Kahn. I realized I would have to do what lots of New Yorkers do when threatened by such as Mr. Kahn. I would have to carry a gun. I would have to carry a gun even in the face of the Sullivan Law, with its harsh penalties for going armed.

In order to carry a gun, I would have to buy one.

34.

The Pakistani will not go away. I am frightened, for he behaves aggressively and is obsessed with me.

I will not stay home at night! I cannot involve the police since it would bring out my acquaintance with Dr. Hoyt and perhaps make trouble for him, even get him deported. I must go on with my life and in order to do that, I have decided to buy a gun and carry it with me when I go out at night.

The problem is, where in New York can I buy a gun with no questions asked? I thought about the problem for a whole day then I remembered Andy Muscatello. Andy worked at Glinzretti Brothers when I was there. He was a foreman on the loading dock and used to work for the juice boys on the side, the loan sharks. He used to get involved in a little strong arm, when it came time to collect.

I tried to think of all the angles. Would letting Andy know I wanted a gun put me under any obligation to borrow money from the Mob? Would he want to know the truth about why I wanted to buy a gun? I thought about it overnight, then I called him. He still works for Glinzretti

Brothers, where it is business as usual, even though the pension funds were stolen.

"Andy," I said. "I want to buy a gun."

He said nothing for a few seconds then he asked why I wanted one.

"Some guy broke into my apartment building and killed one of my neighbors. I want to be ready for him in case he comes back."

Andy said, "Uh-humm."

"Just a small gun," I said. "Maybe a .32."

"I know why you want a gun," said Andy. "Billy, don't do it!"

"Don't do what?"

"Don't go after Angelo!"

"Angelo?"

"He stole your pension, Billy, I know, but don't try to take him out. You'd be bringing a lot of trouble on yourself. Those guys play for keeps, Billy!"

"I'm not going after Angelo! I want a gun to keep in the apartment!"

"You sure that's it? Your not going to try to get even with Angelo?"

"No way!" I said.

"OK," said Andy. "How much do you want to spend?"

"How much? I don't know. What would it cost to get a .32 revolver?"

"A gun like that, about five hundred dollars."

"That much?"

"It'll be fixed so there's no way to trace it."

"Five hundred dollars? That much?!"

"About that."

"OK. Five hundred I can handle. I can't go over that."

"You still got the same phone number?"

"Yeah."

"I'll call you in a day or two."

Two days later, Andy called.

"Go to Washington Square, noon tomorrow. Sit down near the Arch. I've told the guy what you look like. Have the money in cash, in twenties. His name is Frank. He'll find you."

Andy hung up.

By this time, I had changed my mind about buying a gun. I had decided against it. Buying a gun would be foolish. If I bought a gun, I'd just be buying trouble.

I did not go to Washington Square, I never met Frank.

35.

I went to the VA Hospital at 24th Street and First Avenue to visit Herman. They had operated on his eyes to remove the bits of Bernie's teeth and, at first, they had hoped the operation would be successful and that Herman would have some vision. Later, they realized it had been a failure and he would never be able to see again.

I walked up to his bedside and took his hand and greeted him. His eyes were heavily bandaged and he was lying on his back in some sort of harness that prevented him turning over.

"Billy? Is that you, Billy?"

"It's me, Herman. How are you doing?"

Herman started sobbing. "It's so awful! So Goddamn awful!" he said. "Bernie is gone, Billy, gone!"

"I know, Herman, It is awful."

"And they'll never find the one who did it! They'll never get their hands on him! He'll never get strapped in the electric chair!"

"I know."

Herman stopped sobbing.

"They say I'm not eligible for any kind of pension

from Bernie's service in the army," he said. "They said only a legal wife would be eligible to apply for a widow's pension. I'm out in the cold even though Bernie and me were like man and wife for twenty-seven years."

"It's unfair," I said.

"They tell me I can apply for a pension based on my own army service and Aid to the Blind through Social Security. BLIND! Did you hear that, Billy? I'm BLIND! GODDAMN BLIND! Whatever I get won't be enough! What am I going to do, Billy? What am I going to do?"

"I'm in the same boat, Herman. The Mob stole my pension and I'm out in the cold, too. Once what I've saved is gone, I'll be living on Welfare!"

"How could this have happened?" asked Herman, starting to sob again.

There was a black man in the next bed to Herman's. He was sitting up and had heard everything we had said. He was a pleasant man, almost cheerful, even though he had what he called "the cancer".

"Pray to the Lord," he said.

"Herman, is there anything you can remember about the man who killed Bernie? Is there anything you could tell the police, anything that might help them?"

"I've already told them everything," said Herman.

"Everything?"

"All except one thing," said Herman. "Bill, Bernie knew the man. He recognized him, they even talked before he shot Bernie."

"You didn't tell this to the police?"

"No," said Herman.

"Why?"

"Billy, he was a hustler! Some piece of shit hustler Bernie had thrown out of the arcade a couple of times."

"What for?"

"Billy, you know how Bernie ran that place. Any hustler wanting to get in the back, where the tricks were, had to tip Bernie twenty bucks a day."

"And the killer would not tip Bernie? You mean he killed Bernie over a twenty dollar tip?"

"Hunted him down, Billy, that's what he did! Killed him in his own apartment!"

"Why didn't you tell this to the police?" I asked.

"It might have made Bernie look like he was on the take or something like that. It would not have looked good for Bernie!.

"How much did Bernie make from the tips?"

"Lots! Sometimes four hundred dollars a day. Never less than two hundred."

An idea came to me.

"Who did he work for? Do you remember his boss' name?

"Not right now," said Herman. "He was some foreigner."

"Try to remember his boss' name!" I said.

"Billy, I just can't think!"

"TRY!" I said.

"Den'Carno! That's it! Mr. Den'Carno!"

"Den'Carno!" I repeated.

"Den'Carno at the Crystal Arcade! Go see him, Billy! You could get the job! You'd get it in a minute, as much as you know about arcades!"

36.

I called the Crystal Arcade that night and asked to speak to Mr. Den'Carno. I explained to the man who answered the telephone that I was Billy O'Leary and I wanted to talk to Mr. Den'Carno about a job in the arcade.

"He ain't hiring," the man said.

"Tell him I'm a friend of Bernie Aurelio."

In a moment, Mr. Den'Carno came to the telephone.

I told him I was a friend of Bernie Aurelio and I wanted to apply for his job.

"You the guy he lived with?" asked Den'Carno.

"No. He's in the VA Hospital. Blind. I live in the apartment building with them. I was a friend of Bernie's for years. I know the arcade operations, inside and out."

"You ever worked in one?"

"No, but I've been going to them for years."

There was a pause.

"The job's been filled," said Mr. Den'Carno.

"How about I come down and fill out an application? Maybe the job'll open up again."

There was another pause.

"Ten o'clock in the morning. Second floor, Crystal Arcade."

"I'll be there!"

37.

At ten o'clock the next morning, I was at the Crystal Arcade. I went to the second floor, saw a door marked OFFICE and knocked on it. A man about my age opened it and asked what I wanted.

"I have an appointment with Mr. Den'Carno."

The man told me to come in and have a seat. Mr. Den'Carno had someone with him, he said.

After about ten minutes, a door inside the office opened and a man I took to be Mr. Den'Carno came through it and with him was the Maharajah, the blue skinned manager of the Bon Joy. He saw me and said the first words he had ever spoken to me in the ten years I had been patronizing his arcade.

"Good morning," he said. The Maharajah had an English accent.

Mr. Den'Carno took an interest in me when he realized the Maharajah knew me.

"Mr. Den'Carno," I said. "I'm here to fill out an application."

"You need a job?" asked the Maharajah.

"You know this man?" Mr. Den'Carno asked him.

"A long time," said the Maharajah. "He's a regular customer. He did us a favor once, knocked out some nut who was planning to torch the place."

"You knocked out a man?" Mr. Den'Carno asked me, in surprise.

"He's handy with his fists," said the Maharajah.

"I was a boxer," I said. "Middleweight. I was on a few cards at the St. Nicholas Arena, in the old days."

Mr. Den'Carno took me into his office and I sat in a chair in front of his desk. The Maharajah stood behind Mr. Den'Carno. We talked half an hour. When he learned my pension had been stolen, he seemed genuinely sorry.

"So you were a friend of Bernie Aurelio?" he asked.

"Good friend!" I said.

"We think Bernie was killed by someone looking for revenge. Something that happened at the arcade, maybe. He might still be a customer. Does that scare you?"

"No," I said.

Mr. Den'Carno said he had already hired a man to take Bernie's place but he was not sure he was going to work out. If he had to let the man go, he said, he would call me.

"Paul says you're all right!" he said, as I was leaving.

I nodded and left.

Paul, I assumed, was the man I had been calling the Maharajah.

38.

It was less than a week before Bernie and Herman's old apartment was rented to someone else. I could tell he was off center the first time I saw him, but I attached no importance to that because the rest of us in the building were also off center. As a matter of fact, I have always found people who were out of the main stream to be much more desirable as friends and acquaintances than the sort advertising tries to make us into.

His name is Donny Mudway and he works at night, doing something with computers. He is about thirty, thin, even willowy, and has a strange way of moving his hands, sort of like he is miming birds in flight. He works from three p m until midnight and is at home in the day time.

It took him one day to discover me, that is, he noticed that I, too, was at home in the day time, and he started trying to get me to tell him all the horrible details of Bernie's murder. He said it was unlikely the murderer would ever be brought to justice, how unlikely, even if caught and convicted, it was he would ever be punished. We agreed that even if he was convicted and sentenced to die, he would never be put to death, that appeals would take years and years, that he would just stay in jail, ultimately forgotten about, making wallets and religious sculptures out of popsicle sticks.

One day, he asked if I would like to come up to his apartment for a cup of coffee. I pondered his motives. Why would he be interested in me, a man old enough to have been drafted at the start of World War II, and I would have been were it not for the fact that one of my legs is shorter than the other. Maybe he is looking for a father figure, I thought. Why not go up and have a cup of coffee, I asked myself. Maybe he will take Bernie's place and sometimes go to the market for me.

As soon as I was seated in his apartment, he asked if I would like to see him model some "fashions". Uh oh, I thought, Donny Mudway is a drag queen who is going to make me sit here and watch as he dresses in women's panties and garter belts and bras and hose, then make me sit even longer while he puts on make-up and a wig and then gets his rocks off striking poses.

I said, sure, let's see the fashions and he hurried away to the other room and returned in time wearing a long, ground dragging, woman's chenille bathrobe and a pair of carpet slippers you would expect to find on an old lady in a nursing home. He struck a pose, swirled, then hurried into the other room, returning in a long flannel night gown and another robe that looked like it had been made from an Indian blanket. He changed several more times, modeling chenille robes and Mother Hubbard bedclothes and I murmured words of appreciation.

"Aren't they lovely?" he asked, pointing to the robes

and nightgowns he had arranged in a display across the back of the sofa. "Yes" I agreed. "Very".

Donny was the first transvestite I had ever encountered who was fascinated and I presume, titillated, by wearing the unglamorous sleeping garments favored by very old women.

After the modeling session, we talked for a long time and he made coffee and offered me some cookies. He was, I decided, all right, if off the beaten path, and when I mentioned that since Bernie and Herman were gone I had no one to go to the grocery store for me, he volunteered immediately.

39.

They say the most dangerous place in the country is Forty-second Street from Broadway to Ninth Avenue. It may be, but I have not had much bad luck in all the years I have been going there.

One can assume he will be held up, mugged, robbed and even injured, if he goes into some parts of Manhattan, especially at night. The robber will demand your wallet, and if you give it to him with no quarrel, he will usually disappear without harming you. I am talking here about the robber who is a professional, experienced and sane, who just wants your money. I am not talking about one of the crazies, of whom there are thousands, or the drug addict who has lost control of himself.

Back to the wallet. If you walk Forty-second Street at night, you should carry a wallet you are prepared to give up. I buy used wallets every time I go to the Salvation Army thrift store and collect snapshots, which you can also get at the thrift store, to put in them. I find cast off membership cards and those plastic things that look like credit cards which you sometimes get in the mail and I put them in an old wallet and take it with me when I go out at night, leaving my own real wallet on top of my bureau. I have three or four one dollar bills in the fake wallet and I put the money for the night in my front shirt pocket.

Thus I am prepared. If a robber demands my wallet, I will pull out the stage one, look anguished, say something about it having the only photograph I have of my mother in it, and hand it over.

I have been robbed three times. The first time, I was coming home early in the morning, about three a.m., it was, walking up Broadway to my apartment. I noticed a Puerto Rican boy about fourteen years old, come out of a doorway ahead of me and start walking in my direction. I paid no more attention to him. He went out of my mind altogether, and I did not realize he had slowed his pace and actually fallen behind me. I became aware of him again when I felt him at my side and I saw he had a knife and was pressing it against my ribs.

"Give me your money!" he said. He reached into my left hip pants pocket and pulled out the fake wallet. "There's not much there," I said. "I spent just about all I had tonight."

He looked in the wallet, took out the few singles there, threw the wallet to the sidewalk and ran away, around the corner.

The next time I got robbed was inside the Sultan Arcade. A heavyset black man, with a hat pulled down over his face, was walking the aisle in front of the movie machines, back and forth, never entering a booth. He waited until I was the only one not in a booth and pushed up against me and said "Give me all of it!". I was put off at first, not realizing what he had in mind, then I felt a pressure on my side and looked down and saw a nickel plated revolver with a long barrel in his hand. "Give me ALL of it!" he repeated. I was calm. I said something like "You're the Boss!", which I had once read was the proper attitude to take with a robber of the sane variety, and it worked. I reached into my pocket and took out a fake wallet. He put it in his jacket pocket, put the revolver back in his belt, straightened his jacket, and said, "Don't you follow me!" and walked slowly out of the arcade.

The third time I got robbed was just this past summer. It was early on a Saturday night and I was headed toward the Bon Joy when two black streetwalkers approached. "How about a party, Pops?" one asked. I shook my head and said "I'm gay," a ploy that I have often used to get rid of pestering streetwalkers. It did not work this time. They kept on with the hard sell and I realized they were both high on something and not likely to be influenced by my tricks. "We take gay money," one said. "We'll see you get a good blow job!" I then realized they had backed me up against a building. I saw no weapons and I could have floored both of them if I had wanted to but I stayed calm. I knew there might be a pimp watching who would get involved if I flattened them. Then one of them pulled a knife from somewhere and held it against my throat.

Two well dressed men carrying briefcases passed, saw what was going on and looked away.

"We'll just take your money and you can save your load for one of your gay boys," said one. The other took my wallet, another stage one, out of my pocket then they stepped to the curb where an automobile with two men in it appeared and they got in and they drove away.

I have been lucky so far. My little scheme has worked three times but I am no fool. I know that one day I will be set upon by a crazy or a drug addict who will have a mind so cloudy no prepared behavior will move him and I will probably get shot or badly cut. I will go on, anyway. I cannot stop visiting the arcades. They have become too big a part of my life to quit.

Of course, I never reported the robberies. The police have lots of them to catalog and there is no chance the robbers will ever be caught except by accident.

I have given some thought to trying to find a light-weight bulletproof vest or a wide belt of chain mail to wear around my waist.

40.

I have not told you about Grey. Grey is his first name and he lives in my apartment building. He is about thirty-five and works as an orderly at a big hospital and one of his duties is to shave the crotches of men to prepare them for surgery. He uses a small electric razor which neatly removes the hair without pulling, he assures me.

When he shaves off the hair, he does not throw it away, although I am sure the patients assume he does. Instead, he saves it and after leaving the patient's room, goes to his locker, where he stuffs the hair into one of those plastic pill containers.

He labels each one with the name of the patient, his race, and his age. If the patient is a famous person, as many of them are, he so indicates on the container.

Grey has about four hundred containers of pubic hair in his room and he opens one now and then to enjoy the bouquet. He says each one smells different and I have, on his invitation, sniffed two or three, and I can tell the difference, one from another.

He says that he has pubic hair from professional athletes, elected officials, opera stars, famous actors, even heads of state. I looked at the names on the containers and many of them were familiar.

41.

Last night, as I was entering the Bon Joy, I heard a man on the sidewalk in front of it calling to me.

"Sir! he said. "May I speak to you in God's name?"

"No!" I said.

The man was one of the Christian fanatics who are always preaching to people along Forty-Second Street. He was about twenty-six, plump, wearing a suit and necktie and had his hair combed back from his temples.

"God does not want you to go in there and see what is on display!" he said.

"Fuck you!" I said.

"It is not me who is asking you, sir! It is God who is asking you!"

"Fuck the both of you!" I said, as I was joined by another arcade regular, the retired English teacher, who was also just entering and who had stopped to find out what was going on.

We walked into the arcade, past the Maharajah, who remained impassive. I bought ten dollars worth of tokens from him as the Christian continued to plead with me not to.

I pushed past him and prepared to enter one of the booths for a quiet evening of watching men in monocles whip women wearing nothing but German army helmets.

The man grabbed me and tried to stop me physically.

"Why are you bothering me?" I asked.

"God has called me to save you!" he said.

I looked at the display of bondage magazines on the wall and one caught my eye. I took it out of the rack and held it up in front of the preacher, like one is supposed to hold a mirror or a cross to drive away a vampire.

The cover of the magazine showed a naked woman, a full view, frontal crotch shot, with thorns, long thorns, six inch long ones, stuck through her labial folds and with a cord laced between them.

He saw the color photograph and covered his eyes, then turned, trying to get out of the arcade with his eyes closed. He stumbled and fell over a table leg, then got up, his hands still over his eyes, and lurched out into the street, barking his shin on a display case along the way.

The Maharajah caught my eye and smiled at me.

42.

It was cold, about twenty-five degrees, and there was light snow falling, as I walked to the Sultan. I passed two barefooted men lying on the sidewalk. They looked dead.

I stayed in the Sultan about two hours, watching some of the patrons as they coupled in the darkness and chatting with some of the regulars, and listened to them talk about things they had seen there the night before, then I left.

A crowd had gathered where I had seen the two men. I edged into it and saw them sitting up, both alive, their faces twisted with pain and terror.

"What happened?" I asked a policeman.

"Kids," he said. "Some kids poured lighter fluid on their feet then lit it."

43.

There is an Italian restaurant on Sixth Avenue much favored by young men and women who hope to become fashion models. They take tables near the window, where they can be seen by people passing on the street, then sit there, toying with pasta, in costumes intended to look like street clothes. Their hair is stylishly tossed, their teeth are capped, their eyes are bright and no one is over twenty years old. They are on display, always showing their best face, their best smile, hoping they will be noticed by someone who will help them in their frenzied attempt to get work.

Their beauty is astounding and they are all perfumed and clean and desirable.

How attractive would those preening in the restaurant window be if they were forced to go one day without soaps and laundries? How attractive after a week?

Those young women, sitting there tonight, watching the snow fall as they exhibit themselves, those stunningly beautiful women, come here from Iowa and Oregon and Utah to work as models, how alluring would they be after a week without a bath?

44.

Sammy Gloo is a friend of mine who lives on Ninth Avenue. He is Hawaiian, part Chinese, part Japanese, and is about five years older than I am. Sammy is a little man with bad teeth, grey hair and one of those beards found on Chinamen, nothing but five or six long hairs hanging from his chin.

He talks like somebody in a Charlie Chan movie, but he can disguise his voice and sound like a young college boy from the Middle West. He has a bad habit that costs him about three hundred dollars a month, or about a third of his pension from the post office. Sammy likes to call an all male Sado-Masochistic Hot Line on the telephone and talk to the anonymous studs, always pretending to be a man about twenty.

I have been in his apartment when he has dialed one of the 900 numbers and I know he can fool them. After he is connected, he asks, "Is there a Top on the line?" A Top is the term for the sadist or the master. I have listened in on his extension. Soon after he asks if there is a Top on the line a tough voice will ask, "Where you calling from, boy?" Sammy will pick a state, sometimes Michigan, sometimes Maryland. "What's your name, boy?" "Danny, sir" (Or Davy or Roger or Todd) Sammy goes on, leading the Top.

"What have you got on, boy?" "Nothing, sir, except a pair of thick white gym socks."

Sammy talks on like that, making the Top think he is a young good looking college boy, well built with a big schlong, just waiting to be handcuffed and whipped and fucked. The Top will give Sammy his home telephone number, where they can talk in private and for much less than the two dollars a minute it costs to use the hot line, and Sammy will call him and keep up the pretense, even pretending to get his rocks off while the Top is talking about whipping him over the telephone.

I have watched Sammy make one of those calls three or four times and I always listen on the extension. It is all real as far as the Top goes and he actually believes he has a young stud on the line.

Sammy tells me it is all for laughs, a joke on people he will never see or ever contact again. Sammy is always smiling and laughing at the end of each little episode.

I have seen him cry a little, too. He is not fooling me. It is real for Sammy, too. He pretends because he knows none of the Tops would give him a minute of their time if they knew he was a scrawny, one-legged old Chinaman in a wheelchair.

45.

I was dressing to go to the Bon Joy when there was a knock on my door and I heard a voice saying, "Billy! Billy! It's me, Donny!"

Opening the door, I found my fellow tenant Donny Mudway, dressed in the bedclothes worn by old women. He had on a sleeping bonnet of flannel with a floral pattern, a long nightgown and over it, a chenille bathrobe. He was wearing house shoes made of carpet material and had an Indian blanket over his shoulders.

As soon as I let him in, he started talking. "I have a little problem," he said. "I need help and I'll just have to tell you about it and hope you won't throw me out!"

"Go ahead," I said. "What is the problem?" He told me he had been in his bed, fucking himself in the ass with a dildo (he described it and I recalled seeing it on the bedside table one time when I was in his room. It was about eighteen inches long and is sold in the arcades under the trade name The Butt Buster) and had been twisting the instrument while it was inserted and it had broken in two.

"There is an eight inch long piece of it still up there," he told me. "I can't get it out! What am I going to do?"

I told him he would have to go to the Emergency Room.

"No!" he said. "I can't do that! It would be too embarrassing!"

"You've got to go!" I said.

He kept on refusing, suggesting absurd alternatives. I was insistent and told him I would go with him in a cab to St. Elizabeth's Hospital, which is about six blocks away.

Donny agreed but first called the Emergency Room there and got a guarantee from them that he would not be made fun of when he arrived.

We started out, me in my sweaters and overcoat and Donny in just what he had on, the old woman's night clothes and an Indian blanket. I told him he would appear less ridiculous if he put on a pair of pants and a shirt but he refused, so I gave up and we went outside, in the intense cold, and walked up to Ninth Avenue where I hailed a cab. I was uncomfortable because of Donny's clothes, or lack of them, but I realized this is New York and the doctors in the Emergency Room have already seen everything.

"They promised they would get me in and out with no commotion," said Donny. "Very low key, very discreet, they said they would be."

We arrived, I paid the driver and we walked into the Emergency Room. There were lots of people there, waiting to see the doctors. Donny went right up to the admission desk and said in a loud voice, "I'm the one who called! I'm the one who has a foreign object in his rectum!"

The others in the waiting room, hearing Donny and seeing what he had on, probably assumed he was a mental case. He sat down and settled in to wait to see the doctor, but in what seemed like an instant, he was called back to the treatment room.

He returned in about half an hour, all smiles, and said the doctor got it out. The doctor was an older man, according to Donny, who considered his predicament hilarious, and told him a dirty joke while removing the object.

"It seems," said the doctor, "there was a gay fellow walking down the street and he saw a man walking ahead of him with whom he instantly fell in love. He followed the man blocks and blocks until he entered an office building and went up in the elevator, with the gay man still following him. The man being followed got off the elevator and entered an office where the gay man following heard him greeted as 'Doctor'. The gay man noticed the sign on the door: 'Proctologist'. He ran to a telephone and made an appointment to see the doctor the next day. When he was admitted to the treatment room, he told the doctor he had been having pains in the rectum. The doctor examined him and said, 'Here's your trouble! You've got a dozen long stemmed roses up there!' The gay man smiled and said, 'Read the card! Read the card!'

Donny said the doctor took long, thin tongs and put them into his anal cavity, and after a few false starts, got a purchase on the piece of dildo wedged in there and slowly pulled it out.

He held it up, in triumph, with the tongs for Donny to see. "Do you want to keep it as a souvenir?" asked the doctor.

"No thank you!" said Donny.

We got in a cab and started back to the apartment

building. "Did you laugh at the joke?" I asked Donny. "I certainly did not! I thought it was in very poor taste!"

I saw Donny safely to his apartment then I went back out, to the Sultan, walking, as always, through the cold night.

It was a busy place when I got there. All the booths were occupied, and I had to wait a few minutes before I could get in one and look through the hole in the wall to see what was going on in the booth next to me.

First, I saw a white college boy, tall, he was, maybe six foot, seven inches, clutching to him a very short black girl who looked like a high school student. There was no groping, no exposed genitals, they just clutched each other, as tight as possible, while watching the movie. This was boring and I moved over to the peephole on the other side, and saw a man in a bus driver's uniform, masturbating.

I could see someone else watching him through the hole on the other side of the booth. I could not see much, just enough to be sure there was another pair of eyes besides mine on the bus driver.

He had a climax and shot his load onto the floor, then he wiped his schlong with his handkerchief, zipped up his fly and left the booth.

Immediately, the man who had been watching on the other side left the booth he was in, entered the one just vacated by the bus driver and got down on his knees and licked up the still warm semen off the floor.

46.

I walked home from Forty-second Street last night in
a freezing rain. It was bitterly cold. Near Ninth Avenue
and Forty-fourth Street, I passed a woman sitting on the
sidewalk with her back against the wall of a building. It
was Polly, sort of a celebrity as street people go, and she
was holding out a cup, begging, as usual.

Polly is a thin, dirty, toothless old hag, who always
wears a red bandanna around her head. She is famous for
being discourteous to everyone, even those who give her
money.

"Can you spare a dollar?" she asked me, as she pulled
a blanket tight around her shoulders. I have known her for
at least four years, meeting her for the first time one summer night on Madison Avenue. She asked for a dollar then
and I ignored her and walked on. As I passed, she yelled
at me, "Fuck you!"

I put a few dollars in her cup. "Fuck you," she
screeched after me.

When I got home, my heavy black wool overcoat was
stiff with ice. I hung it on the shower rod so the water
would drip into the bathtub as the ice thawed. Sometimes,

I wonder if I should not stay home when the weather is this bad. I wonder, but I always go out, anyway, even in weather worse than this, because the lure of the arcades and the breathless thrill I get there are always too great to act sensibly.

Once I took off my coat and my jacket and my sweaters, I started having a chill. I stood against the radiator to get warm, then, feeling like I was coming down with a fever, I took three aspirin tablets and got in bed, under my Salvation Army blankets.

I went to sleep easily but at once I started dreaming, the hectic, feverish dreams of one getting sick. I dreamed I was in jail but I did not know why, then I dreamed I was very hungry and visions of food started racing across the picture screen of my mind.

Soon, I went into deeper sleep. I realized I was breathing heavily, and then I had another dream.

It was dark, night time, the hour at which I am always on the street and it was very cold. The chill came right through my clothing. I realized the sidewalk was deserted. The lights of the city were shining but there were no people, no automobiles, no movement at all.

Thick snow started to fall. At once, the sidewalk was covered, the street was covered and there was no path to follow, no beaten down snow, nothing to guide me.

I walked a block or so and then I saw forms, shapes on the sidewalk. I got closer and realized the forms were street people, sleeping there, six or eight, no movement coming from the shrouded mounds. Then I saw one of the forms sit up and pull a blanket away from its head.

It was Polly, even more gaunt, even more unappealing,

the red bandanna around her head, a smile on her face. She beckoned to me, come, she said with her arm, come lie beside me, come here and I will cover you with my blanket.

I was terror stricken. She continued to beckon to me and pointed to a snow free spot on the sidewalk, continued inviting me to lie beside her, to share her warmth.

One by one, the other shapes on the sidewalk removed the blankets from their faces. They were the fashion models I had seen in the Italian restaurant on Sixth Avenue, still young, but now dirty, their hair uncombed, their breath foul.

Each looked at me, then pulled his blanket over his face and went back to sleep and was soon covered with snow.

That is all I remember. I woke up after that and discovered I had fever. I got out of bed and took two tablespoons of NyQuil and went back to bed.

I awakened at the usual time, feeling all right, no fever, just hungry. I got dressed and went outside. Everything was covered with two inches of ice. It was hard to do, but I walked down Ninth Avenue to the Studio Cafe, for breakfast.

Outside the cafe, I bought a copy of the TIMES and went in and sat down next to Sammy Gloo and ordered pancakes, sausage, butter, honey and hot tea, very, very hot tea. I told Sammy about my acute hunger and he said it was a symptom of diabetes and pointed to where his legs had been amputated.

A headline in the TIMES caught my eye.

MOB FIGURE SLAIN. ACCUSED IN PENSION THEFT. FOUND DEAD IN NEWARK.

I read the article. It was Angelo, all right, shot at a park picnic table.

Sammy took the TIMES from me and read the article.

"Is this the one who stole your pension?"

"Him and others," I said.

47.

There are a million dangerous mental cases wandering the streets of New York City. You encounter one practically every time you leave your home.

One day last week, I decided to take the subway to Battery Park then the ferry to Staten Island and back, just to see the Manhattan skyline. I got on the subway at the Fifty-ninth Street Station and sat down beside a young man. I did not pay much attention to him, there was nothing notable about him. After a few minutes, he touched my arm and said, "What's going on, Doc?" I responded in a general way and he said, "You don't remember me, do you?" I looked at him closely, noticing the vacant eyes, the spindles of teeth and said, "No, I don't." "You're that doc, the one who told that judge I was crazy!" he said. "It wasn't me!" I said. "You're him, all right," said the young man. "You're him, just older and gone to fat."

He took a knife from inside his jacket, pressed the switch and the blade sprung out. He started whetting the blade against his shoe sole, as I looked around at the other passengers. None of them had noticed the man. I was sure from my knowledge of New Yorkers that none of them would come to my aid if he started to attack me.

I slowly put my right hand into my overcoat pocket and clutched the role of nickels I always keep there, then, slowly, I brought my hand out of the pocket and sat there, waiting to see what was going to happen.

The motorman called out the Forty-second Street station and the man rose, put the knife back in his pocket then got up and stood by the door, waiting for it to open. He looked back over his shoulder at me and said, "I'll see you later!" and mimed taking the knife out of his pocket, pressing the switch, and then he slashed the air viciously, several times.

He got off the car, laughing like a mad man.

48

The hopeless beggars I tolerate and sometimes give money to them. The ones I despise are the arrogant, healthy ones who seem to have all their marbles, who stand at intersections, holding out cups, and demand that you give them money.

I was in the Village and an old man, more or less clean, more or less sane looking, asked me for a handout. I told him I did not have anything to give him.

He drew back a fist and said, angrily, "You know you got a dollar!" "Don't you threaten me, you son of a bitch!" I said and I prepared to flatten him. He cooled off and began to walk away, but I would not let him off so easy. I took his shoulder and turned him around and said, "You need to work on your approach!"

Recently, I was walking on Fifth Avenue in the day time and came upon a young man holding up a small girl about five and the man was calling out, "We need something to eat! Help us get something to eat!"

Everyone ignored him.

49.

Two plain clothes detectives from the New York City Police Department called on me this morning. They knocked on my apartment door at seven a.m., and when I opened it, they showed me their identification and asked if they could come in and talk to me.

Of course, I let them in.

Their questions were general, at first. Are you Billy the Gimp? I am Billy O'Leary, I said. Did you work at Glinzretti Brothers? Yes. Were you one of those whose pensions were stolen? Yes.

Then they got to the point.

We got a tip that you bought a gun to kill Angelo.

I shook my head. I've never bought a gun in my life, I said.

The detectives, whose names were Landis and Gebauer, asked if they could look around the apartment. With my permission, they opened a few drawers, looked under the mattress, hoping to find a gun.

"Your union business agent was murdered and you are a suspect," said Detective Landis. He gave me his card. "Call me first, if you plan to leave town."

"Call us if you hear anything that might be of interest to us," said Detective Gebaurer.

They left and I locked the door behind them.

Their tip came from Andy Muscatello, of course. I guess he was never told I did not show up to buy the gun he had arranged for—what's his name—Frank, to sell me.

50.

Today, I saw myself ten years hence, on the street. I saw a man, thin, well-born, with a neat grey mustache, dressed as well as a man can be, tweed overcoat, green felt hat, grey suit, a maroon vest, subdued necktie, medallion toe shoes, walking against the flow of traffic on the sidewalk. He had a small sack from one of the drug stores in his hand and was frantically pushing his way through the crowd.

Patent medicine, I am sure, was in the sack. He looked ill, even feverish. He had gone to the drug store to buy medicine and, after the fashion of his class and period in history, had dressed up to do so.

I saw myself in him, though I am not thin, not well-born in appearance, and never has my clothing been as coordinated as his was. Still, I saw myself, alone, ill, forced to go out in the cold to buy cough syrup or antibiotics, alone in the world, stumbling against the flow.

51

I had wandered into a sex aid and novelty shop in the Village, located on two floors of one of the old buildings there. Downstairs, in what had originally been the basement, they had the usual sexual gadgets to be found for sale in any such place. An old black man was the sales clerk.

Upstairs, they had more of the same plus a selection of provocative underwear and nightgowns. The sales clerk there was a good looking young Puerto Rican girl, who could not have been over eighteen. I looked around, found nothing of interest and was getting ready to leave when the telephone rang and the girl answered it. Something told me to stay there and listen.

The conversation was unfocused, at first. "Yes, this is the Reality Emporium! Yes! I'll be glad to help you if I can". Soon the girl was saying to the one on the telephone, "Well, no, I've never actually used one myself!" After that, I listened with delight, while pretending to look at dirty magazines.

Someone on the other end of the line, a man who had told the sales girl he was twenty and to whom she confessed she was only seventeen and too young to legally work in such a place, was getting off over the telephone by talking to her about the uses of her merchandise.

Essentially, the man on the telephone was making an obscene call, but how could you fault him when he was talking to a girl who sold cock rings and tit clamps. She was having a good time, without even realizing she was being used, or exploited, as the Women's Libbers would put it.

"Oh, that sounds like a lot of fun!" she said, at one point.

They were arranging to meet when I left. I never had such a good time listening to a telephone call before in my life.

He had told her he was twenty. I wondered if he was really another Sammy Gloo, a burned out old man in another wheelchair, who had a young-sounding voice. It could actually have been a twenty year old or even a fifteen year old.

Whomever he was, whatever his age, I thanked the Fates for allowing me to share his call.

52

It is nine o'clock in the evening. It is snowing out and very cold. The weatherman said it will probably set records, the low temperature we can expect tonight. He said it will be colder than the lowest recorded temperature for this date, which was in 1932 when it fell to six degrees below zero.

I will not risk the walk to Forty-second Street on a night like this.

My room is warm, there is a small light behind my chair and I am having a little supper, sandwiches and a cup of tea.

The streets are deserted, there is no noise, just the occasional passing taxicab. I finish the sandwiches and put a record on my turntable, James Melton, singing songs from PORGY AND BESS.

I doze in my chair, a really big chair, a Morris chair, with the metal rod in the back that lets you adjust it. I bought it at the Salvation Army years ago. Some who have seen it say it may be valuable, maybe a Morris chair made by William Morris, himself. I do not think it possible and anyway, I love the chair too much to think of selling it, because I can doze in it without my legs going to sleep.

On these very cold nights, when I am well fed and snug in my apartment, when I am coming in and out of sleep, I usually think about Pauline.

Pauline was a woman I first met almost thirty years ago. She was twenty-two then and was a call girl who was hooked on speed. She was good looking, with short blonde hair, good teeth and a nice smile, when we first met, but the drugs pulled her down quickly. She was on the street next, then fell even below that, to working as a stripper at a dyke bar.

She got busted for drugs, was sent to the women's prison at Dannemora then came back to town on parole. I used to see her around. Sometimes, I would loan her a few bucks, sometimes I would buy her lunch and we would talk about things but we never had any action together. I lost track of her for fifteen years and then, one night, I ran into her in Times Square.

Pauline was much heavier, even fat, but relaxed, off the dope and she told me she had gone to school to become a beautician and had a steady job and an apartment off 35th Street.

She was glad to see me, I could tell, and I was happy to see her. We talked awhile and soon we got to discussing some action. She said it would be fine with her and since she had quit the streets, it would cost me nothing.

We took the subway to her apartment, walking to the station through snow falling softly in big flakes. Her apartment was a two room affair on the fourth floor of a building dating from the 1880's, with a Korean hat wholesaler on the ground floor.

As soon as we got inside, Pauline took my hat and coat and started running water in the bathtub.

"What's with the bathtub?" I asked. "I'm going to give you my special treatment" she said. "The one I save for special friends."

She filled the tub with very hot water then poured some bath oil in it. Pine, it was, a wonderful scent like fresh sawed wood and turpentine and the way they say it smells in the mountains.

I got in the tub, taking a long time to get used to the hot water, and Pauline started bathing me with a soft wash cloth, not to get me clean, but in a sensual way, even massaging the back of my neck with her hands.

She left me in the tub, telling me to relax and enjoy the pine scent and the safe and soothing feel of the hot water while she made up the bed. I did as I was told and slipped down in the water until the back of my neck was under it and I sort of dozed off, thinking, I remember, what a lucky man I was to be here at this moment.

I must have slept for five minutes then I was awakened by Pauline, holding a bath towel and telling me it was time to get out of the tub. She dried me, rubbing the towel vigorously against my back, then patting me dry elsewhere.

She took my hand and led me to the bed. Flannel sheets! There were flannel sheets on the bed, cotton flannel, like my mother put on my bed when the nights were cold and the house not too warm.

Pauline took off her clothes while I was under the covers. She was overweight but she looked good to me, exactly like those classic Rubens nudes, and she had great, proud breasts and dark areolas around the nipples. She got in bed with me then reached over to the phonograph and put on a record. "I just love this one" she said. It was *I'm Looking Over a Four Leaf Clover I Overlooked Before* by Art Mooney and his orchestra. She pulled me close to her and I put my arm around her and we listened to the record and when it was over she turned off the phonograph and drew her thigh across my belly and we kissed and made love and I have never known a warmer nor more affectionate woman before. She was just sweetness itself, and comfort and security and I felt snug and happy and knew I belonged there.

We got together often after that, always, it seems, on very cold nights and there were always the flannel sheets, pulled tight and the pine scent and the incredible warmth.

She went to visit her mother in Arizona about five years ago and never came back. On nights like this, I remember Pauline and wish she were here.

53.

I have mentioned Grey, the hospital orderly. I want to tell you more about him because he is the most cheerful man I have ever met. He is always Up, never depressed, never unhappy, always smiling, usually almost dancing, in some sort of pixie fashion.

When he is not upstairs in his room, sniffing the little containers of pubic hair he has shaved from surgical patients, he is out looking for action. He is the most avid seeker of gay sexual encounters I have ever met. He sometimes goes to the arcades along Forty-second Street but not often because working one, that is, waiting around for people to come in, takes too much time.

He prefers certain department stores and he knows where to find the action in most of the colleges in New York City and in the museums and galleries.

Grey will sit for hours in a booth in a mens' restroom, a booth with a good size glory hole in the wall between it and the booth next to it, and sometimes give twenty blow jobs in a single afternoon.

He carries a large shopping bag with a pair of shoes in it, shoes markedly different from the ones he is wearing as he enters the restroom. After sitting there for an hour or so, he will change to the shoes in the shopping bag, so that any authority figure will look at the man in the booth and conclude it is not the fellow who has been in there the past hour.

Grey carries several packets of sugar, those small, single serving ones you find in restaurants, and before he settles into a booth for an afternoon of relaxation, he will sprinkle the sugar all over the floor near the door of the rest room. Anyone trying to slip in and catch him performing a sex act on another man will step on the sugar and make enough noise to warn him.

He uses the shopping bag to carry his spare shoes, and when he gets someone in a booth with him, he will ask him to stand inside the shopping bag—which is very large—so it will look, to a store security officer, like one man in the booth, with a bag of his purchases.

Grey carries a mirror and a flashlight and has been known to disguise himself with a wig and fake mustache.

54.

I have described the movies shown at the Bon Joy, a high class arcade where the quality of projection is excellent, the color good, the focus perfect and the sound level just right. There is no person to person contact in the Bon Joy, the booths have no glory holes in them nor are there any peepholes. It is all strictly business there, just good clean dirty movies with no contact between the patrons.

Then, there is the Sultan, which I have already mentioned, and where it is intended patrons have contact with each other. The place is dirty, it smells like air freshener and industrial floor cleaning compounds. The booths are made of plywood, and have not just peepholes, but large openings between them, big enough to squeeze through, one to the other. The screen where the movie is shown is just a white space on the door and it is always covered with messages written by the patrons. Sometimes, the screen will be so cluttered with writing—often, in wide felt-tipped pen—that it is difficult to see the movie.

These messages are such as, LET ME FUCK YOUR WIFE; HEAVY HUNG STUD WANTS TO FUCK YOUR WIFE. Sometimes you see SLAVE WANTS MAS-

TER and there are the replies, BE HERE SAT 15TH NOON or sometimes just telephone numbers.

The quality of the projection at the Sultan is very poor. Sometimes, the machines do not work at all, often the picture is fuzzy. No one objects, for no one comes to the Sultan to see the movies. They come to meet others and have sexual relations on the spot.

Every Saturday night, a couple comes in to the Sultan at about eleven p.m. He is in his fifties and wears a suit and a hat. She is near forty and always wears a fur coat and fishnet hose and high heel black shoes. They go into one of the booths that has a large hole on one side of it, opening into the next booth.

Once inside, she takes off the fur coat and is revealed to have on nothing but the stockings. She and the man wait until another man gets in the next booth and when he sticks a hard schlong through the opening, the man will feel it, test it, as it were, and if he approves, he will slip a condom on it and the woman will back up to the booth, bend over, and take it from behind. If the man in the other booth tries to fondle the woman, the man with her will slap his hands and push him away. All the man in the other booth is allowed to do is get his rocks off and usually it takes very little time. The man in the other booth leaves and is replaced by another who is waiting in line outside the door. If the man with the woman finds something wrong with the man who enters the other booth, such as a tiny schlong, or a dirty one, or if he is drunk or wants too much action, the woman will put her fur coat back on and they will start watching the movie in their booth, waiting out the man in the other booth, sometimes as long as thirty minutes, until he gets the message and leaves and is replaced by another.

The couple stays in the Sultan two hours or more and in that time, the woman will have serviced ten to fifteen men.

How do I know this? The Sultan has two levels and if you stop on the staircase leading to the second level, and lean way over, you can see what is going on because there are no tops on the booths. On any night that the couple is in the Sultan, there will be six or seven men on the stairs, leaning over, watching.

I do not know if the couple realizes they are being watched. They probably do and it probably adds to their happiness.

There is another type of arcade, which I call The Big Operation, a good example of which is the Crystal, where I went to call on Mr. Den'Carno. I never spend much time there, it is just too busy, there are too many employees, tough looking guys who may be armed. I hear you can get drugs there and it is a place where rough hustlers hang out. I have seen some of the young Puerto Rican girls who perform in the sex shows there. They are pretty but have hard faces.

55.

There is a man, not as old as I am, with red-grey hair and bushy red-grey eyebrows, who cleans up the Sultan. He comes to work early in the morning, when there is not much business, turns up the lights and sweeps out each booth then mops the floor with a disinfectant.

He is from the south, Georgia, I think, and he may be retarded, although I am not sure, since I have not talked to him that much.

Walt is his name and he lives, or at least sleeps, in an empty booth at the Sultan. I have looked inside his room, or the booth where he lives, when he has the door open. There is a mattress on the floor in one corner, a chair, a small television set and a radio.

He is always trying to get a blow job. He will sidle up to anyone he things may be interested and say, "You can have it if you want it". As far as I know, no one has ever wanted it.

Sometimes, I envy Walt. He has a place to sleep and a small income and works among people who are there for a good time.

56.

I was chatting with some of the regulars at the Sultan last night, and one of them, a man whom I think is a Professor of Chemistry at one of the colleges here, said he was walking through Times Square a few nights ago, when a young black boy, fourteen at the most, came up to him and said, "Will you fuck me in the ass, White Master?"

57.

There are many lovely Japanese women in Manhattan.
You see them on the street, coming toward you, and
you imagine they are drenched in a perfume made from
cherry blossoms and when they pass, you find it is true.

58.

The most bustling city in the world comes to a stand-still whenever there is a really heavy snow storm. The only two times the city is quiet is when there is a snowstorm and at three o'clock in the morning.

It is snowing heavily tonight. In hours, the city will be shut down. It will be quiet and cold, the snow will deaden all sound, and blind people who depend on sound to make their way will be baffled and many will get so depressed they will commit suicide.

I am putting on my sweater, my jacket, my black over-coat, my gloves, my overshoes, my scarf and my hat and I am getting ready to go to Times Square. I will start out walking. I am in good shape, from walking to Forty-second Street every night and I should be able to make it with no trouble since the snow is not yet deep. If I have a time of it, I will get a taxi.

Once there, I will not go to the arcades. On snowy nights like this, I go to a restaurant I know of on Forty-first Street and order a big bowl of bean soup with sausages and hot rye bread and dine alone at a table, while watching the young actors and actresses who gather there.

They have come here from the other cities, from Dallas, and Cleveland and St. Louis, where they appeared in local productions of GUYS AND DOLLS and HARVEY and A STREETCAR NAMED DESIRE and they are not yet cynical, not yet weary and they have bright and happy faces.

59.

M'Liss found a French cookbook at the Salvation Army and in the past three weeks she has used it to prepare the following gourmet entrees:

Brains in White Wine; Baked Brains in Bacon Rings; Creamed Brains; Sauteed Brains in Lemon Sauce; Brains en Casserole; Brain Salad; Sauteed Kidneys: Kidney Creole; Kidney Patties; Kidneys with Sour Cream; Chicken Fried Beef Heart; Beef Heart Loaf with New Potatoes; Beef Heart en Casserole; Sauteed Beef Heart; Sweet and Sour Lamb Tongue and Creamed Tripes.

60.

The first Hollywood film star I ever had a crush on was Ann Sheridan. I used to whack off while looking at photographs of her in movie fan magazines.

I also enjoyed looking at photographs of other actresses, among them Evelyn Keyes, Gloria Graham, Paulette Goddard, Joan Bennett and the French star, Michelene Prelle. There were actors, too, whom I found it exciting to think about, now and then, and among them were Tab Hunter, Lon McAllister and Peter Lawford. I used to keep a color photograph of Peter Lawford, wearing white sox and loafers with tassels, within easy reach.

There were others, names I cannot even remember now, and others who were not famous, just real people I saw on the streets or with whom I worked, whom I found attractive and exciting.

They were as nothing compared to the only real obsession I have ever had in my life—Edie Sedgwyck.

It was Andy Warhol in whom I first became interested. I heard from someone I met on the street or in one of the arcades, that he, too, was a foot fetishist, even badgering women, and presumably men, too, he met at parties to let him draw their feet. I thought at first of writing him a nice letter and asking if we could compare experiences. After all, it is not easy to find just the right foot and I thought he might be able to give me some tips on where to look for them. I did not write Andy Warhol, for I realized even before I sat down to, that it would be absurd. He would not respond and there I would be, having opened myself to a stranger.

Instead, I started hanging around in the street in front of what he called The Factory, hoping to catch him leaving or maybe, just coming outside for a breath of air. I saw him once, coming out of the building with Edie Sedgwyck on his arm. I discovered her and forgot all about him.

She was the most vibrant woman I had ever seen and at once, I was smitten. I set out to learn all I could about her, I continued loitering in the street near The Factory but now, hoping to see, perhaps even meet, Edie Sedgwyck. I started collecting pictures of her. There were lots of them around, for she was modeling for VOGUE and there were photographs of her to be had by writing The Factory. I read about her in the newspapers and saw her in the news-reels and I put two framed pictures of her on the wall of my apartment.

Edie was a very troubled young lady at this time, drugs, mostly, and perhaps just craziness in general, but I did not know it. All I knew was she was part of a Bohe-mian crowd such as I had always ached to belong to. I closed my eyes to the fact that all the young people I saw coming in and out of The Factory seemed scroungy in the extreme, all clearly mental cases. Whenever Edie met a stranger, she would say, "Let's fuck!". That was all I wanted to know.

She thrilled me! That was it! Here was a glamorous, rich and beautiful young lady who ignored the rules, who scoffed at the taboos. I actually got to know quite a lot about her by accosting the dregs of humanity who were part of Warhol's studio and who worked with her. Once, I stopped a dirty, emaciated boy with a bandanna around his head and the eyes of a dope fiend, who was leaving The Factory one night and I casually asked him, "What's Edie up to, these days?". He was stupefied with drugs, himself, but said she was "whacked out" and that she had moved into the Chelsea Hotel.

I called the office at Glinzretti Brothers early the next day and arranged to take my two weeks vacation, beginning at once, and I went to the Chelsea and registered as a guest. Edie always wore black leotards and a long shirt, and she stood out in a crowd because of the costume and because she was ethereal, in general. Once I got settled at the Chelsea, I asked around and found out her room number and then walked the hallway in front of her door, every day, for as long as I dared. It was like living in a madhouse, being at the Chelsea. There were the long time residents, the painters and composers, who kept to themselves. Then there were the young ones, the writers, the poets, the would be rock stars, who lived at the Chelsea, hoping that some of the creative spark left behind by earlier residents might rub off on them.

I used to sit in the lobby for hours, hoping to see her coming or going. Once, very late at night, she came in with two men, both drugged out of their minds, and she passed as close as two feet from me, and got in the elevator. I used to see her leave sometimes in the late morning, going to The Factory, I guessed, and she always had on those trademark black leotards.

It was near the end of my two week stay when she set her room on fire. I was in the lobby when men from a private hospital came for her. She saw me standing there, as they were leading her out, and she stopped and smiled at me and said, "I am going away!".

I thought my heart would stop beating.

A biography of her came out after she died and I read it through, in one sitting, and learned she had been disturbed since early childhood and never really had any chance at all.

One of the photographs in the biography ended my obsession with her. It was a picture of her dancing, barefooted, in a long gown.

Her feet were long and bony and almost ugly.

I was free!

Edie Sedgwyck was my last infatuation. Since I see so much female nudity every night on the arcade screens, it is almost impossible to be aroused by the sight of a naked woman.

Now, I am aroused by the sight of a provocatively clothed woman and I have found the best source for photographs of this sort is the L L Bean Woman's Specialties catalog.

61.

For the past three nights, I have had the same dream. I find my neck and chest covered with blood and then I discover it is seeping from my left temple.

How long do I have before I die? How long before I wake with a pain in the leg which they will find to be cancer? How long until I lose the leg? How long before the cancer reappears as a growth on my back?

How long do I have before there is evidence of a malignant growth on my jaw bone? How long before the jaw has to be removed and a new jaw-like object made of slivers of my thigh bone has to be fashioned and set to graft against my skull?

How long before I notice blood in my urine? How long before I have a stroke?

I think it will be a long time. I will stay well as long as I continue to go to the arcades. I watch the movies there to keep from dying.

62.

Sometimes, I go up to Sixth Avenue and Fifty-sixth Street to watch the streetwalkers. There are streetwalkers elsewhere, but I like to watch the ones on Sixth Avenue. They are young girls, some black, some white, wearing short skirts and high heeled shoes, even on winter nights. They stand at the corner and openly accost single men who pass by. They always get a polite response, either "OK" or "No, thanks". Sometimes, they walk alongside young men, trying to interest them.

I once saw a very young streetwalker take the arm of a young boy from the South and ask if he wanted to party. He looked at her, embarrassed, then said, "Your tits is pretty!" She asked him if he had any money, and he said "No, ma'am". "Then shove off, Baby Butt Face!" she said, and pushed him away.

Many times, I have seen a streetwalker take a man's arm and walk a ways with him, and I will see him take out his wallet and look in it to see how much money he has.

I think they try to get one hundred dollars for a quickie, as they call it. It must be dangerous work, going to rooms with strange men, the odds being that one out of every twenty men in New York is a dangerous psychopath.

These woman are always good looking, although sometimes I notice an older one, past her prime, standing around the corner. I somehow have gathered that these older women must be some sort of supervisor. I am sure the girls all work, directly or indirectly, for the Mob. Sometimes, I see a sinister looking man in a Cadillac parked on the street near the corner where they are working. I have even seen the man call one of them over to the car for what looked like instructions.

Although the women openly solicit for business, even standing out in the street, addressing single men in cars when they stop for the traffic light, there must be an occasional arrest made by the police, for I have heard two or three times one of the women yell out to the others, "The car!" and they all scurry away, into buildings, on the side street, when a police patrol car drives by.

They all look healthy although I cannot see how they could be since I have seem them thinly clad on snowy nights.

Could it be true that they are all in some sort of bondage to the Mob? That is what one hears. One hears that they are all drug addicts, at the mercy of tough guys who take their earnings.

They notice me, standing in a doorway, and sometimes, one will come up to me and ask, "Want to party, Pops?" and I will smile and say "Not tonight".

63.

Frankie Rosenthal is the nearest I have been to having a girlfriend. We met in the mid-Forties, when I had been out of high school about three years and when she was already working in a dress shop on Madison Avenue.

She is retired now, after thirty-six years as a sales lady in Gimbel's basement.

In the old days, we were very close. We used to go to the movies, the grand theatres on Forty-second Street, and once in a while, she would spend the night in my apartment.

We were lovers, and maybe, even, in love. Sometimes, I thought we were. We might have married, her father liked me well enough, but the Rosenthals were Jewish and he did not want—would not permit—Frankie to marry a Gentile, especially an Irish Catholic.

Frankie never married, either, and so we have both grown old alone, but keeping in touch, seeing each other now and then.

I took her to dinner last night. It was her birthday and we went to the Old Garden Restaurant on West Twenty-ninth. We used to slip into the Old Garden for a quick supper when we were younger and she was at Gimbel's, which was near by on West Thirty-third Street.

The Old Garden has been there in the same spot, in the basement of an old brownstone, since around 1890. Nothing has changed; inside, it still looks like it did the day it opened and I understand the same family still owns it.

My father and mother used to have dinner there in the Twenties. My father told me he once saw Mayor Jimmy Walker and his girlfriend Betty Compton dining with some gangsters, one of them being Arnold Rothstein, the man Damon Runyon wrote stories about, the man he called "The Brain".

When I got to the Old Garden last night, Frankie was already there, waiting for me at a table under the arches, on the far right wall.

Frankie stayed thin, she never had to worry about what she ate because it never made any difference, she was always about one hundred and thirty pounds. She has been dying her hair for years, keeping it a deep red-brown. She was wearing a brown wool dress, a brown cloth coat and a pair of sensible shoes, the kind you associate with guards in a womens' prison, or retired Gimbels sales ladies.

She smiled when she saw me and stood up as I approached the table. I took her in my arms and kissed her on both cheeks then we sat down and the small talk began.

"Happy Birthday!" I said. "How many is it, now? Twenty-six?"

She laughed and I asked if she had been waiting long. "Not long" she said.

I looked at Frankie's hands. Her fingers were stiff, her hands closed in half fists. I touched her hands. "Arthritis?"

I asked. She nodded her head. "Sometimes, it's worse than other times. They don't hurt so much tonight".

"Is it just your hands?" I asked. "My knees, too," she said. "I'll be eternally grateful to the government, or whomever is responsible, for fixing the street corners so that the handicapped do not have to step down off the curb."

"Handicapped? I hate to think of you as handicapped!"

We ordered dinner. I had an appetizer, chopped liver with onions and crackers, Frankie got chicken soup. The food was good and we smiled at each other, then they brought us the entrees, me a chicken breast stuffed with ham and Swiss cheese and mashed potatoes with chicken gravy, and Frankie, baked chicken with rice.

It was fun, talking to her. We always got along so well.

She said something about it being cold in her apartment, how she wished she had someone in bed with her to keep her warm, then she came out and asked, "Why don't you come home with me, tonight? Spend the night. In the morning, I'll make you French toast, with apple butter, like you like it."

"You'll be disappointed," I said.

"Disappointed?"

"It doesn't work anymore."

"Doesn't work?"

"I can't get it up anymore."

"Have you been to a doctor?"

"Sure. There's nothing they can do. Old age. High blood pressure, the medicines I have to take. They've killed it, the medicines, and the fact I was born so long ago."

"What about one of those operations? What about an implant?"

"I've tried the shots. Testosterone, a shot in the hip. No help."

"I mean surgery," said Frankie. "I've heard they can remove a testicle and replace it with a rubber ball you squeeze when you want to get it up. What about that?"

"That might work," I said.

"You ought to see about it! You're too young a man to have to give it up. Find out if there's something they can do!"

"I'll look into it."

Frankie toyed with her dessert. It came with the dinner. I got a strudel, she got a chocolate sundae.

"We're just to old, Billy."

"That's it! Just too old."

I took her hands in mine and massaged them softly.

"We're just playing out," I said.

"How did it happen?"

"How did what happen?" I asked.

"How did we get in this fix? Both of us, old, almost too old to care for ourselves. No children to look after us, no friends. Two old people, facing the streets alone, trying to keep our independence until that day they put us away in some home. How did it happen?"

I stroked her hands, ever so softly.

"We just missed out," I said.

"Missed out. Everything passed us by."

"We just missed out," I said, again.

The waitress brought us another cup of coffee and we

lingered, then I paid the bill and we walked out of the Old Garden, onto the street. It was cold, snow was falling.

We went to her apartment on Thirty-ninth Street and watched a little television then got in bed and snuggled together and watched the snow fall, outside the window.

In the morning, she made French toast and I ate four pieces with apple butter and I had three cups of coffee and a glass of orange juice.

Frankie told me her sister in Hoboken, now a widow, had invited her to move in and she was going to do it.

"Hoboken? That's not too far away," I said.

"Just across the river."

"We can still see each other."

"Of course!" she said.

We said goodbye in mid-morning and by noon, I was back in my room, listening to music.

64.

Are you repelled by my life style? Are you disgusted by my amusements? Which of the arts would you suggest I substitute for what I am enjoying?

The musical play? I have already seen THE FANTAS-TIKS. There are few other musical plays worthy of my time. There is no Kern, Gershwin, Rodgers and Hart, Lerner and Lowe, no Irving Berlin. There is only Stephen Sondheim and Andrew Lloyd Weber. Between them, they have written only four or five songs you can hum in the taxi on the way home from the theatre.

Poetry? It is a lost art. I have already read all the real poetry there is. That being written today fails to raise the goosebumps.

Painting? There are probably lots of paintings being created that I would like to see but I will never get to, for the taste-makers will never hang them.

Sculpture? Another lost art. Have you seen that wrought iron wall at the Javits Center? Have you seen the famous clothes pin and the famous umbrella? They are examples of the trivialness of our times.

The motion picture? Ah, yes! But, specifically, the pornographic motion picture, and within that category, I prefer the subclass dealing with bondage and discipline and worship of the foot, subjects so arcane there are few examples to be found, except in specialized houses.

I have found my art form.

65.

The Mob is efficient.

You will remember, I told you about my fellow tenant, Bud, who made good money on the side, whipping people in his apartment, Bud, the clam manager at a seafood restaurant, who witnessed the murder of a mobster in the private dining room.

They found Bud's body yesterday, covered with snow, behind the bus station on West Forty-second Street. At first, the people who pick up the bodies every morning thought Bud was just another anonymous street person. Then they found identification on him and a wallet with six hundred dollars in it, and they noticed he was young and wearing good clothes.

They looked closer at Bud's body and found a few bullet holes in him, the main one being in his forehead.

What bad luck! Doing his job, opening clams, minding his own business, when two killers enter the back door of his restaurant.

Bud would have kept his mouth shut! The Mob could have depended on it.

66.

On the way down Eighth Avenue last night, I stopped, for some reason, and just listened to the sounds of Manhattan. Living here all my life, I have grown accustomed to the noise and do not even realize it is there.

Stop and listen to Manhattan.

The first thing you notice are the incessant sirens, a firetruck or ambulance, or police vehicle, one or the other of them is blaring every minute of the day, on top of which there are the sounds of traffic, the honking of automobile horns, the squealing of brakes, the clanging of loose manhole covers.

And the voices, the people, the languages, the foreigners, the Haitians, Japanese, Koreans Puerto Ricans. You can stop and listen and not hear English spoken.

I think I am the only American in New York.

67.

There is a shopping mall on Long Island which has five upscale womens' shoe stores. It is possible to sit on a bench outside the entrances and watch everything that goes on inside.

I go there and watch young girls try on shoes and I thrill at the sight of their smooth, pink feet. Sometimes they wear thick white socks and sometimes they try on boots and I watch it all, sometimes sitting there for an hour at a time and no one ever notices me.

I am cautious, however, and when I think I may have been sitting outside one store too long, I move on to another. I only sit in front of stores that cater to young girls in the sixteen to twenty range. I avoid the stores that serve older women, even though they may be rich and elegant, for I am not excited by calluses, bunions and hammertoes.

Last Saturday, I sat down in front of a store that sells mostly boots and at once I saw a sight I will remember forever. It was the woman I noticed first for she was wearing jeans that were a little tight and had long red hair and a face you associate with happiness and good times.

She was trying on a boot, pulling at the top, trying to

get her foot in it, with the leg of her jeans pulled up to her knee. She got the boot on her foot and hobbled toward the man, whom I had not noticed until that moment.

He was nearly fifty, trim, with a grey mustache and long grey hair swept back over his ears, a retired military man, perhaps, or a merchant seaman, for his face was bronzed and roughened by the outdoors. He smiled at the woman and asked if she liked the boots.

She sat down beside him and started to pull the boot off her foot. She struggled with it and at last it came off and I saw she was not wearing hose or socks, which I had always thought was against the rules that go along with trying on shoes.

Her foot was not smooth like those of the young girls, but her toe nails were painted red and her foot was as exciting to see as an older woman's can be.

I looked at the man again, he was smiling in a way that could only mean he was buying her the boots, made of soft, black leather that came up past the knee, for her to wear when they were alone.

68.

M'Liss Cameron-Pease quickly went through her "Interest in Hunger" phase and enrolled in a graduate School of Social Work, where she planned to specialize in Sex Starved Children, a subdivision of Child Abuse.

There, she learned about Ego Strength and was told by her instructor that persons with low self-esteem acted out their impulses. She concluded pretty fast that I had low self-esteem as evidenced by my regular attendance at the adult movie arcades.

"It's plain and simple, Billy" she said to me. "If you had any self-respect, you would be going to regular movies, like everyone else, and not to those dirty movies that degrade women!"

Regular movies, indeed! For me, the regular motion pictures ended when W C Fields died, when Gary Cooper died, when John Hodiak died. I have been to some motion pictures in recent years and found I did not like them. I want the movies of the old days, movies like STAGECOACH, directed by John Ford, not the second version. The first STAGECOACH had one of the best lines I ever heard in a movie. Claire Trevor is a fancy lady being run out of town by the puritan women there. She is on the stagecoach when it stops in the middle of nowhere and picks up John Wayne, "The Ringo Kid", who has just escaped from jail. Wayne sits beside Claire Trevor and tries to get better acquainted. She high-hats him. John Wayne finally gives up and says, "I guess a fella can't break outa jail and into society all in the same day!"

Of all the movies I remember from the good old days, when movies were an escape, as the intellectual snobs called them, my favorite was JOHNNY EAGER, with Robert Taylor, Lana Turner, Van Heflin and Edward Arnold. Van Heflin won the Academy Award for Best Supporting Actor that year, for his performance as Robert Taylor's alcoholic friend. I was fascinated by the concept of Johnny Eager, as played by Robert Taylor. Eager was an ex-convict, who posed by day as a cab driver. By night, he was the crime lord of the city, living in sumptuous apartments at a racetrack. The picture ended with Eager in a gun battle with other gangsters, on a dark street, a street of warehouses and second hand clothing stores.

Today's movie faces mean nothing to me. Where are the great character actors of today? Where are today's Edgar Buchanans? Dub Taylors? Florence Bateses? Josephine Hulls? Percy Kilbrides?

M'Liss found a support group, a self help program conducted by one of the professors at the School of Social Work she was attending, and insisted I join it. I was able to fend her off for a few days but she is a demon and I finally gave up and agreed to go to a meeting with her.

The next night, at about seven-thirty p.m., M'Liss and

I were in a taxi heading to the YMCA on Sixty-second Street, where the group met. It was snowing heavily and the taxi moved slowly through the nearly deserted streets. M'Liss was babbling about how much I would gain from the session and I was fuming inwardly, I wanted to kick myself for getting into this situation.

We arrived and M'Liss insisted on paying the cab driver. The meeting was to be held in a small room on the ground floor and when we got there, eight people were already seated around a table. They all rose when we entered and M'Liss said to them, "This is my friend, Billy!" and one by one, they came up to me and introduced themselves. They said things like, "I love you, Billy!" or "You're top drawer, Billy!" or "You're First Class, Billy!"

We all sat down and awaited the arrival of the group leader, a man whose name I learned was Lepanto. Just Lepanto. It was all first names, only. As one of the women there said to me, "We all love each other, so its just first names!"

Lepanto entered. It was all I could do to keep from laughing. He was a short, dirty looking man with a ratty beard containing food particles. He wore a necklace of bear claws and Birkinstock sandals with dirty white sox.

He greeted the group, excessively upbeat, I thought, and led them in a rousing, "We love you, Lepanto!" Then he opened the briefcase he was carrying and took out an aerosol spray can of RAID insect killer and sprayed it all over his body, his hair, even his face.

I was baffled and whispered to M'Liss, "What in the Hell is he doing?" She replied in a whisper, "He says there are bugs everywhere he goes."

It was sort of like an Alcoholics Anonymous meeting. Each rose and said, "My name is Floyd and I have no self-esteem" or "My name is Gloria and I hate myself." After each such confession, the group said in unison, "We love you, Floyd!" or "We love you, Gloria!". Lepanto acted as sort of a cheerleader, urging the group to be even more sincere in its claims of love.

Lepanto stopped for a coffee break. I had observed him eat two large boxes of a cheap candy called Sweet Tarts, while conducting the meeting.

When he left the room, one of the women there came over to me and reintroduced herself. "I'm Wilma and I love you, Billy!" Wilma was about ten years younger than me and slim and well dressed, including soft grey leather pumps with a two inch heel. She had on a perfume I recognized but did not know the name of.

I took her seriously, like the fool I was, and said something harmless, thanked her and then casually asked if she would like to go to dinner some evening.

"With you? I should say not! I have a boyfriend and he's a doctor!"

Lepanto returned to the room about that time, his locks dripping bug spray and eating from a fresh box of Sweet Tarts. He led the group in another, "We love you, Lepanto!", to which he replied, "And I love you, each and Every One!"

I got up and walked out, having to first shake M'Liss loose from my sleeve, who insisted I stay, saying, "Billy, you need what Lepanto has to offer!"

Outside, the snow was falling even heavier. I walked down to Fifty-ninth Street and took the subway to Forty-second Street. It was about a three block walk from the subway station to the Bon Joy but it seemed longer because I was so eager to get there and because the snow was deep and had drifted high in places.

The Bon Joy was open, brightly lit, cozy and warm, and the Maharajah, whose name I now knew was Paul, was at his place at the counter, impassive as usual, and said nothing as I bought a few dollars worth of tokens.

I hurried back to the viewing booths, entered my favorite one, fed a handful of tokens into the slot then I kept pushing the selector button until I came to one where Erica is whipping Irmagarrd with a telephone cord and I told them about my evening and how awful it was and how people are such weaklings and I did not leave out anything and I especially gave them all the details about Lepanto, what a mental case he was and I asked them why people like him are not more often seen through.

They did not reply for they had no answer.

69.

There is a young man named Gribble who lives with his mother in one of the apartments in my building. His mother is around seventy and is confined to a wheelchair and requires a feeding tube inserted into her stomach through the nose in order to take nourishment. A visiting nurse comes to the apartment every other day to check on her and be sure the tube is in place.

When her son goes to work, she is left alone, although M'Liss looks in on her three or four times a day.

Yesterday, I was in my apartment, dozing, for I had been at the Bon Joy until three a.m., when M'Liss knocked on my door and called out, "Billy! Come quickly!" I opened the door and there she was, very excited. "Mrs. Gribble's nose tube has slipped out and her son needs our help to get it back in!"

I hurried with M'Liss to the Gribble apartment and found Mrs. Gribble in her wheel chair, with her son standing over her in a dressing gown.

"Please, mother!" he said. "Please just cooperate! I've got to get to work! I have an appointment to frost Mrs. Gelder at two o'clock!"

I could see that the tube had slipped out of Mrs. Gribble's nose and that her son was trying to reinsert it, despite the old lady's strong objections.

"M'Liss! Billy! Can you hold mother down while I insert the tube?" asked the son.

"No! No!" said Mrs. Gribble.

"Mother, you've got to have the tube in your stomach so you can get food!"

I could see a can of diet supplement and a funnel at hand, with some packets of prepared liquid food. I already knew the son fed his mother during the day by pouring the liquid into the funnel and it ran down, through the tube, into her stomach.

Mrs. Gribble continued to resist efforts to reinsert the tube.

"Mother! Do you want to starve?"

"Yes! Yes!" said Mrs. Gribble.

"M'Liss, you hold her head steady. Billy, you hold her hands," said the son.

M'Liss looked perplexed. "Shouldn't you wait until the nurse can get here?" she asked the son.

"I know what I'm doing!" he said. "I'm a licensed cosmetologist!"

We held the old lady still, M'Liss holding her head in her arms and me, holding her hands. The son inserted the tube, in what appeared to be a very competent, swift motion and we relaxed our hold on the old lady.

"There, mother!" said the son, "It's all over!"

The old lady looked at her son with eyes narrowed to slits and said, "I hate you, Hershel!"

70.

Once in a while, I do a little business with the hustlers who lean against the wall in the shadows, along Eighth Avenue, but only if I run into one who looks sane and who is small enough for me to count on being able to beat up, if things get out of hand.

I was on the way home last night, walking up Eighth Avenue. At Forty-fourth Street, I saw an attractive boy in a doorway. I slowed down, our eyes met, I stopped. He asked if I knew what time it was. I told him, then I asked if he had had any luck.

"Some," he said.

"Are you looking for a little action?" I asked.

"Are you a cop?"

"No," I said. "Are you?"

"No," he said.

We talked some more, his purpose in standing there was now crystal clear, so I asked his price.

"It depends," he said.

"How much for a blow job?" I asked.

"Forty-nine ninety-five!" he said.

"How much to let me see your toes?"

He pondered that one a minute, then said, "Twenty-nine ninety-five."

I complimented him on his aggressive price structure then told him I would have to catch him next time.

71.

Mr. Khan, the man I have decided is from Pakistan, had been following me every night. I had grown accustomed to him. Perhaps familiarity breeds contempt, for I had become less cautious and had almost decided he was harmless.

Saturday night, however, as I walked up Eighth Avenue, he followed me closer than ever and was actually muttering threats.

When I reached the Bon Joy, I enter and he followed me inside, the first time he had ever done so. I bought the tokens and started into a booth. He then made his move, he rushed into the booth ahead of me and pulled me in, his hands around my throat as he spat out the words, "You killed my sister!"

I gave him the old knee in the balls and he let me go. I hit him in the face as hard as I could with my right fist and I could hear the cartilage in his nose cracking. I kept punching him, the face, the ribs, back to the face. It was almost like being back in the St. Nicholas Arena.

Mr. Khan slid to the floor, unconscious.

I went out in the lobby to tell Paul there was a man

passed out in one of the booths, but before I could say anything, he said for me to go on home, that he would take care of it.

He smiled, as if to acknowledge I had skillfully handled a problem.

I left the Bon Joy and walked down the street to the Sultan. I still had all my tokens and I spent an enjoyable evening, talking to a few of the regulars, and watching a few sexual encounters in the booths, perhaps the most interesting being a tall college boy who whacked off while watching a woman have oral sex with a small pony.

I walked home, feeling free of Mr. Khan, who it appeared was not an agent of Dr. Hoyt, after all, but simply one of the thousands of mental cases in the city.

72.

Mine eyes have seen the Glory!

College boys masturbating in the darkness; black couples screwing; old men being fucked in the ass; naked boys kissing and discovering themselves; anorexic streetwalkers giving blow jobs to fat boys; boys rimming middle aged men; girls together, kissing and fondling each other; older couples, married probably, watching the movies and cuddling; transvestites, truck drivers in drag, their blue jowls hidden by make up; girls using a long dildo with a head on each end, screwing each other, gasping and panting; other voyeurs; toe suckers, and those who lick up semen from the floor; girls in handcuffs, clamps on their nipples; big penises, tiny, minuscule ones; big tits, heavy and striated, and the tits of school girls, pert and firm; girls with rings through their nipples and men with rings through the head of their penises; cock rings; French ticklers; whips; leg irons; fisting; girls with tattooed buttocks and near naked women getting fucked by a series of men.

These things I have seen while crouched in the darkness, peering through holes in walls.

73.

By now, you will have read enough of this narrative to have noticed the tight sentences and the stately language, and you have probably asked yourself how it is that this stamper of pickle jar lids, who never went past high school, could do it.

I have had help and now is the time to acknowledge it. I write out my thoughts in longhand on a yellow legal pad and give them to Alvin, the disbarred lawyer, who edits it, adding here, taking out there. He then gives it to M'Liss, who types the final manuscript, adding her own language whenever it seems called for.

Early on, M'Liss asked me why I was going to all the trouble of writing about myself and I told her I was doing it because I wanted those who come after to know that there was a Billy O'Leary who lived in Manhattan and for the most part, had a good time.

Alvin said I should tell the readers what I look like.

Easy. I looked like an old motion picture actor who was in a lot of movies in the Forties, and who played a Spanish guerrilla leader in FOR WHOM THE BELL TOLLS.

I look like Akim Tamiroff.

74.

The peace others find in solitude or in the Cathedral comes to me in adult movie arcades. If I am worried about getting old, about my money being gone, about coming down with cancer, if I am depressed by the absence of family, children, grandchildren, if I am frustrated by rejection, all I have to do is walk through the neon-streaked darkness and enter the nearly true darkness of an arcade and at once, I feel all my problems vanish, I feel tightened muscles relax and I feel my blood pressure going down.

There is the same sense of festival I have often sensed at resorts, where everyone there has come to have a good time.

Never mind the crazies you sometimes encounter, never mind the smell of urine, the floors sticky from old semen, never mind the smell of sewage, the arcades are my sanctuary.

75.

I went to the Whitney Museum on Madison Avenue last Sunday to look at their Hopper, the one titled, I believe, Sunday Morning, the one showing the face of a block of tenement houses. I find it almost as Holy as I do the adult arcades and other Hopper works I have seen have the same impact on me.

While there, I visited some of the other rooms and came upon a group of thirty people touring the museum with a guide to explain things to them.

The guide, a thin, older man, had stopped the tour in front of an enormous painting, perhaps ten feet by twenty, elegantly framed and hanging in a conspicuous place. The painting was a piece of canvas painted black, the whole thing black, black, entirely black.

"Some people have looked into this painting and seen in it the horrors of the Holocaust," said the tour guide to his charges, and there were murmurs of solemn agreement or revelation from the group.

I look upon such "art" as simply a con game, bogus, all pure junk.

Take that big sculpture in front of the Javits Center,

that long curved wall of cast iron. That is not Art, that is Nuisance!

I saw in the newspaper a few years ago that someone who worked for Leo Castelli, the art dealer who is responsible for encouraging so much of the dreck that is called art today, was killed when a piece of sculpture made by the same blacksmith who made the piece in front of the Javits Center fell over on him.

What an insult! "He died when a free form sculpture fell on him."

76.

I was on my knees no more than fifteen minutes, watching a construction worker, in a hard hat, give a blow job to a man I think is a fashionable Presbyterian minister with a church uptown.

When it was over and I tried to get up, I could not. I could not make my legs work. I was stuck on my knees. Panic came over me, I started getting symptoms of claustrophobia and my heart was racing. I put my hand down on the floor behind me, to see if I could give myself a boost, but my hand slid on a pool of semen and I fell over backwards my legs under me. I managed to reach the latch on the door and pulled it back. The door opened slightly and I saw Jimmy standing near and I called him over and told him I was stuck on the floor.

He got some help and I was rescued.

I have known Jimmy since the early Forties. He was an insurance salesman then but he lost that job and the next one and the next one and even the next because he had the worst luck of anyone I ever knew. He was always getting caught, always getting his name in the newspapers.

Jimmy has what may be the biggest schlong I have

ever seen and I can remember one night back around 1946, it was the night Joe Louis knocked out Billy Conn the second time, me and Jimmy and some other guy who also had a big schlong were in a room at the old Leon Hotel, with a window trimmer named Jerry. Jimmy and the other guy with the big one put their schlongs together and Jerry sat down on them, taking them both at the same time. Jerry had been warming up by stuffing the large end of a hard maple Louisville Slugger baseball bat up his ass and prancing around the room with it hanging out and calling it his tail.

Jimmy has had his lean years, he had a stroke and now walks with a slight limp but he is always cheerful and always remembers me.

"What are you doing so dressed up, Jimmy?" I asked him. "Why are you wearing a suit and tie in the Sultan?"

"I'm working," he said. "I just stepped in here for a little break."

"Working? What kind of work can you do this time of night?"

"Computer programs," said Jimmy. "I deliver them and call on office managers. I've got to see fifty-two before morning."

"What office is open at night?"

"Plenty! Hospitals. Truck Lines".

"Are you making any money?"

"Mucho! Half my customers are closet queens! They buy from me because I let them go down on me when I come calling."

Jimmy waved goodbye and started toward the door,

limping, and I noticed his right arm seemed to be twisted up against his body.

There were some of the regulars there, standing around the Coke machine. After a while, one of them spoke up. It was Morgan, another old-timer, who is a retired Professor of English from some college in New Jersey, run by the Brothers.

"You talk about using blow jobs to sell, there's this guy in my apartment building. A big, ugly son of a bitch, about thirty. Big, rough hands, clumsy as you can get, and what is he but a drag queen!"

There was a lot of laughter.

"He tells me," said Morgan, "that he has this lover who sells stuff to doctors, travels three or four states around here, calling on hospitals, doctors. This guy tells me he goes with his lover on calls, all dressed up in drag, make-up, hose, high heels, wigs, perfume, lace panties, the whole thing. When the salesman gets into a doctor's office, he takes this guy, his name is Wallace, in with him, in high drag, and Wallace gives the doctor a blow job. Wallace says the doctors are always glad to see his lover, the salesman, because he brings them a little treat."

"How in Hell does anyone have the nerve to walk around in drag?" asked one of the others. "Especially, if he looks like you say Wallace does?"

77.

Mr. Den'Carno, the one I had talked to about a job in the arcades, called me this morning. He said he wanted to see me in his office in an hour. He said he had an opening he wanted to talk to me about.

A job! A job! He was planning to offer me a job!

I was there on time and was promptly called in to his office. Paul was there. Mr. Den'Carno started the conversation.

"Paul thinks you might be the man we're looking for," he said. Paul nodded his head in agreement. "He has suggested we give you a chance at running the Jock Haven."

My head was spinning. Me? Running the Jock Haven? I was almost delirious but I managed to stay calm.

"I'd like to have the chance, Mr. Den'Carno," I said.

"Paul says you're in his place a lot, you know the type operation we run and he says you're pretty good at taking care of yourself."

I nodded.

"We'd like you to start Sunday night. We need you on the night shift, from seven at night until six in the morning. It's a long shift. Do you think you can handle it?"

I nodded.

"Six hundred a week." said Mr. Den'Carno. "Can you make it on that?"

I nodded.

"We're a good company. Good salary, good hospital insurance, good bonuses."

"It sounds perfect!" I said.

"Play straight with us and we'll play straight with you. If you get arrested, we'll handle all the red tape, bail, legal fees, fines, things like that."

Mr. Den'Carno offered me his hand and I shook it vigorously.

I stopped at a desk outside his office and filled out a personnel form and an income tax withholding slip, then walked back to my apartment.

All the way home, I felt like I was floating.

78.

I now regretted I was such a loner. I very much wished I had someone to share my excitement with, someone to tell the good news, but there was no one.

It was time to celebrate! I shaved, dressed up, sort of, put on my hat and coat and took the subway up to Fifty-fifth Street and went into the Carnegie Deli for a pastrami sandwich. I go to the Carnegie once in awhile, when there is something to celebrate. I always order too much food and always feel bad about doing it because there is always a hungry beggar or two outside the door.

A lot of famous people go to the Carnegie Deli, especially comics. I was shown to a seat on a bench alongside strangers. I had not been there long when I learned they were tourists from Michigan, in the Carnegie to gorge on one of the giant sandwiches and in hopes of spotting Woody Allen.

I ordered the pastrami and when it arrived, I started in on it, hoping this time to be able to eat a whole one. All around me, people were being served enormous sandwiches and enormous desserts.

The mountains of cheesecakes and sandwiches and

pickles and potato salad were almost too much. It seemed slightly obscene, but I liked it.

I finished the sandwich without seeing any comics or famous people. All I saw were tourists from Michigan, hoping to see famous people. I think I was the only New Yorker there.

As I was paying my bill, I asked the cashier, "When is the best time to see famous comics in here?"

"Anytime! That man who paid just ahead of you—him—there—outside—in the loud coat—that's Henny Youngman!"

I grabbed my change and hurried outside.

"Mr. Youngman!" I shouted at the man. "Hey, Mr. Youngman! I got a job today!"

Henny Youngman looked at me and said, "That's your problem!" and got into a taxi.

79.

M'Liss Cameron-Pease has had another bit of bad luck. You will recall, she got out of jail where she spent ten days for splashing white paint on a fur coat being worn by Mrs. Winston Monaghan, and told us at a welcome home party that she was no longer interested in animal rights because she had found another interest.

She had become interested in Hunger.

That interest did not last long, no longer than it took to discover that Hunger results when people have no Food.

After she wearied of Lepanto and his group, she started going to the meetings of a new thought cult called the First Light Center and began a program there to experience what they called Rebirthing, while floating in a tank of hot salt water.

She tried to move along too quickly, according to the director of the First Light Center, too quickly, indeed. "We told her to wait until she was further along!" she said.

M'Liss tried to walk barefooted across a bed of red hot coals, something the director of the Center said she could do with no ill effects, and burned her feet so severely they may have to be amputated.

80.

Today is my birthday. Sunday, I start to work at the Jock Haven.

As if to honor me, the Heavens sent down a thick blanket of clean snow to hide the ugliness.

I walked through the falling snow, through streets nearly deserted, until I reached Forty-second, which was ablaze with neon and welcoming warm lights. I entered the Bon Joy, nodded to Paul, stood by the rack of bondage magazines, looking at the covers until I was warm, then I bought ten dollars in tokens and walked back to the row of booths.

There were only three others in the arcade, one old man, who probably came in to escape the cold, and a young couple, probably down from Yale for the weekend, handsome people, entwined together as they looked at the posters in front of the booths.

I have said it was my birthday. I entered a booth, locked the door behind me, and took a small, one layer cake, white inside, with white icing, from a parcel I had carried in, then I put one candle in the center of it and lit it. Then I inserted a few tokens in the machine and sat back to enjoy my birthday.

It was Dr. Hoyt on the screen, still wearing his green suit, still drawing arcs and curves on his drawing board while a naked woman, her hands tied over her head and her feet tied together, awaited his attentions.

"Dr. Hoyt!" I said. "You're too much the perfectionist! Will you please just get busy with the work at hand."

And that was how I spent my birthday, perhaps the happiest I can remember, in a warm arcade, alone in fact, but sharing the evening with friends I had made on the screen, Dr. Hoyt, Erika, Wanda, Elsa and the others, while outside, the snow, which I have always considered my friend, was wrapping the streets in beauty.

81.

I am sitting in a chair at a window in my apartment, looking out on the street. The room is dark and it is two o'clock in the morning and very cold outside. The street is deserted and the only movement I can see is the build up of the snow in deepening banks.

Usually, I am in the arcades this time of night, watching as the lonely, often young, often beautiful, meet, touch and embrace, but tonight, I am staying in my room because it is too cold, there is too much snow, to risk the walk to Forty-second Street.

I have a record on the phonograph. Patty Weaver is singing MY SHIP by Kurt Weill and Ira Gershwin. On nights like this, when I must stay at home, I sit in the dark and listen to Roberta Sherwood and Jane Olivor and Barbara Cook and Janis Ian.

The whole town is quiet, shut down. It is easy to imagine that I am the only one awake at this hour, that eight million people are asleep, as I watch over them. Eight million people, most of them frightened, many wicked, many insane, many cold, many hungry, most confident there is a

Providence that will protect them from each other and from pain and from death.

I forgive them for their vanity, and I bless them as they sleep. I pardon the virgins, I smile upon the lovers, I stand beside the old and the feeble and the forsaken and I weep for the dying and the undiscovered dead.